DAYBREAK

ALSO BY MATT GALLAGHER

Empire City

Youngblood

Kaboom: Embracing the Suck in a Savage Little War

Fire and Forget: Short Stories from the Long War (Editor)

DAYBREAK

— A Novel —

MATT GALLAGHER

ATRIA BOOKS

New York   London   Toronto   Sydney   New Delhi

ATRIA
BOOKS

An Imprint of Simon & Schuster, Inc.
1230 Avenue of the Americas
New York, NY 10020

Copyright © 2024 by Matthew Gallagher

First Atria Books hardcover edition February 2024

ATRIA BOOKS and colophon are trademarks of Simon & Schuster, Inc.

For information about special discounts for bulk purchases, please contact Simon & Schuster Special Sales at 1-866-506-1949 or business@ simonandschuster.com.

The Simon & Schuster Speakers Bureau can bring authors to your live event. For more information, or to book an event, contact the Simon & Schuster Speakers Bureau at 1-866-248-3049 or visit our website at www.simonspeakers.com.

Interior design by Jill Putorti

Manufactured in the United States of America

1 3 5 7 9 10 8 6 4 2

Library of Congress Cataloging-in-Publication Data
Names: Gallagher, Matt, author.
Title: Daybreak : a novel / Matt Gallagher.
Description: First Atria Books hardcover edition. | New York : Atria Books, 2024.
Identifiers: LCCN 2023013930 (print) | LCCN 2023013931 (ebook) |
ISBN 9781501177859 (hardcover) | ISBN 9781501177866
(paperback) | ISBN 9781501177873 (ebook)
Subjects: LCGFT: Novels.
Classification: LCC PS3607.A4154415 D39 2024 (print) |
LCC PS3607.A4154415 (ebook) | DDC 813/.6—dc23/eng/20230410
LC record available at https://lccn.loc.gov/2023013930
LC ebook record available at https://lccn.loc.gov/2023013931

ISBN 978-1-5011-7785-9
ISBN 978-1-5011-7787-3 (ebook)

To Anne

Vanity plays lurid tricks with our memory, and the truth of every passion wants some pretence to make it live.

—*Lord Jim*

DAYBREAK

I

The bus pitched east through midnight black and Luke Paxton sat with his head against the window, alone with his thoughts. Winter clawed at him through the glass but he kept himself nestled against it. He found the tinges of outside cold bracing, and wanted to keep awake. He wet his throat and stared out at the flurries of snow dusting the road. Dark, baleful forest lay beyond. A convoy of supply Humvees crested a small hill, pushing the other way, toward the border. Something sharp and hot swelled in Pax's chest. Haven't felt like this in a long time, he thought. It was thrill. It was fear. More than anything, Pax felt like someone again.

They'd crossed an hour before. First had come potholes, then bunkers and checkpoints with barrels of fire licking the night. The checkpoints were for show, performative, barely better than nothing and maybe not even that. Men with flashlights and slung hunting rifles, a gesture at presence for the sake of itself. What they need, Pax thought, is razor wire. Some Hesco barriers, staggered to force vehicles into a funnel. A machine gun on overwatch ready to snuff out any runaways and squirters. The basics.

They'll learn, he thought. It's all new here.

The bus slowed over an old bridge, reaching a village. Brittle Ukrainian sounded through a loudspeaker, reminding of the national blackout. At a bend a tiny church glowed dim, a mural of Jesus holding a candle charting through the snow. Pax blinked and blinked but the image stayed with him long after they left. He hadn't believed for many years but still wanted to be a person who could.

Across the aisle, Lee was draped over his assault pack, snoring away with the clean conscience of a man who knows his place in the world. Pax had dressed to blend in, jeans, a simple black jacket. Lee wore a hoodie with a skull superimposed in front of crossed rifles, the word "INFIDEL" screaming above the logo. He'd raised the sleeves to his elbows to show off his tattoos of flames and razor wire and old unit crests. A nametape and subdued American flag patched across his assault pack, completing the look. When Pax had teased him about it at the airport, Lee had dug in: "I'll be the only Asian around for a fucking thousand miles. People need to know they're dealing with a killer."

He wasn't, though, that was the whole thing. Lee's kill had eluded him through all his deployments, always seconds late to the firefight, a hesitant lieutenant at his shoulder, or a vexing, oblivious civilian standing between him and his chosen glory. It was just luck, happenstance, like so much else in combat, but Lee hadn't been able to shake the sense of lost purpose in the homeland so now he was here, to again carry the gun.

"We gotta be there, man," Lee had said when he'd reached out over the phone, trying to find a travel partner as crazy or bored as he was. "They need people like us."

They? Us? Open questions. Pax had said yes since no one else would, he'd heard it in Lee's voice, something between despair and disgust, and because he'd had no reply for Lee's next line, delivered with all the subtlety of an ice pick: "What else you got going on?"

Pax had another reason for coming, too, one all his own, one that had little to do with this strange new war. He guarded this secret, protected it, had it buried deep in a notebook in the backpack between his feet. It'd been given to him ten years before and he'd held on to it ever since. A lifetime ago, he thought. When I'd been worthy of it. When I'd been worthy of her. The feeling in his chest swelled again. He tried to keep it there. It faded away.

From the rear of the bus, laughter crackled like burning wood. It was followed by amused hushes, which in turn yielded more laughter. Pax knew its source: young Ukrainian men returning from abroad to join the fight. Lee had chatted up the ones who knew English while they'd driven through the outskirts of Krakow, and learned they were a collection of students and IT workers living in the Nordic states. None had a day of military training. The leader, a tall blond kid with high cheekbones, hadn't liked it when Pax interjected to ask what they thought they could contribute.

"This is our country" was all he'd said. He'd said it coiled, with hostility. Pax hadn't meant anything with his question. He'd just wanted to know.

He turned and looked at the group. They were sharing a flask, all coltish energy and banter, trying to conceal whatever was going on inside them with noise. Which is what young people facing the prospect of battle must do. It was the way of things. This was not the time for much thinking.

I'm walking proof, Pax thought, smirking. I know just when to turn off my brain and ignore that I'm washed-up and broken. Pax was thirty-three. He'd been out of the army for more than a half decade. He didn't actually believe he was washed-up. He was less sure about the broken part. His snoring friend was thirty-nine and had quit a job as shift supervisor at a regional electronics retailer in Southern California to come here. They weren't near as close to Corporal Luke Paxton and Staff Sergeant Han Lee of the 173rd Airborne, U.S. Army infantry, as they'd needed to pretend they were to get this far, to be on this bus, rumbling into an alien unknown. Stopping to consider that, or anything at all, would've paralyzed them.

Pax took a slow yoga breath and rubbed at the prayer beads wrapped around his wrist. A lady at the VA had suggested these habits to him, once upon a time, and they worked, not always, but enough. His attention pushed out the window again but there was nothing there for him now, only the void of passing night.

"Sleep. Drink. Watch the dark. These are the options."

Pax followed the rasping words across the aisle. Two rows in front of Lee's slumbering form, a woman leaned over the back of her seat, elbows out, angled toward him. She wore an olive puffer jacket and had pulled her mousy brown hair back into a ponytail, a wave of stress lines running the horizon of her forehead. A shining blue eye the shade of a robin's egg severed the space between. Under the dim lighting of the bus, he could just make out the drooping eyelid that fell over its twin. Pax had taken stock of her earlier. She'd been, and remained, the only woman on the bus.

"And talk," Pax said, sliding over to the aisle seat of his row. "That's another option."

"American," the woman said. "Most of your people are going the other way."

Pax smiled. Doing something different pleased him. "For what are we born if not to aid one another?" he said, repeating a line Lee had posted to Facebook that had earned many likes.

In contrast to the young men, the woman's English was precise, confident. She'd lived in Ohio for a year, she explained, during her studies. Between that divide and a mention of children, Pax allowed himself to relax into the conversation. She's not beautiful, he thought, watching her good eye shine. Not that he could judge much on the matter. He knew he wasn't handsome. Time had given him the face he deserved. Though the rules weren't the same for women and men. It's not fair, he thought. But what is?

"Where are your kids now?" he asked.

"They will stay in Poland with my sister until the war's over." The woman sighed, then corrected herself. "Until the victory."

"Why—" Pax hesitated. It was a tricky question, he knew. But martial law demanded only Ukrainian men stay in-country. "I mean, if you're okay sharing. I'm just a guy on a bus."

"It is my duty," she said. "I'm a military officer."

"Of course," Pax said, hoping he'd masked his surprise, knowing he hadn't. He asked what type.

"NATO countries call it civil affairs. I'll be back east in a couple days. My commander gave me leave to escort my sons to the border. We live near Kyiv, and we knew they'd strike there. They need the river . . ." She trailed off.

Pax asked the name of her hometown. A place called Bucha, she said. Nothing special. Just a quiet suburb.

"I was in the army, too," he said. She nodded as if she'd known that all along. "Can I ask why you joined?"

She laughed. It was the ironic laughter of reluctant soldiers everywhere. "To change the world," she said. Then her voice turned sincere. "It was Maidan. It was the only important thing which happened to us. It showed ordinary people can fight the big strongmen and win. I was too young for the barricades but my brothers and their friends went. They were my heroes. When they came home to rest I'd pour them tea and sneak them my father's beers and listen to what they'd done and seen that day. Their table stories were like magic to me." She shrugged through the dark of the bus. "Besides, my father swears we're descended from Cossacks. Probably not true but families need their little lies."

Maidan. Strongmen. Cossacks. Pax was familiar with these things in a hazy, malleable way, but didn't want to betray the vastness of his ignorance. None of it was why he'd come. The officer saved him from any of that by returning his question: Why had he once enlisted?

"Wish I could remember, fuck," he said, then, "Apologies," because he'd been trying to curse less. His boss at AutoHut had told him it was unprofessional, low-class, that the real world wasn't like the army, and while Pax had resented him for it, the criticism lingered. The Ukrainian didn't seem to mind, at least. She didn't even blink.

"Wasn't patriotism or anything," he continued, rubbing the stubble around his chin. "More like, a way to do something. I grew up in a small town, middle of nowhere. Biggest, nicest buildings were the Methodist church and the National Guard armory." He paused, remembering. "Still think about that, sometimes."

"And why are you here?"

Something seemed to curdle in the recycled air of the bus, and the woman's good eye fixed on him like a shaft of light, the bad one falling away into the shadows. There was a directness to her rasping voice now, a sense of inquiry beyond the scope of conversation. Should I say that I'm looking for someone? No, he decided. Even through the duloxetine, Pax heard silent bells of caution.

"Wish I could remember that, too" was all he said.

He stretched back in his seat, as if to get farther away from the officer. From the corner of his eye, he saw Lee awake, watching them both with a glancing stare.

———————

About time he stopped with the jabbering, Lee thought. Everyone knows who we are and why we're here. Let that be enough.

Lee again checked his wristwatch. The hour had changed at the border and the old compulsion to inspect and reinspect his equipment simmered within him. His girls hated this tic but without it, where would they be? Down a few jackets and hats, for starters. He wasn't flush with money. He didn't have the resources to buy them new outfits every other week. And his fucking ex-wife, forget it. That woman was helpless. He had no idea how they'd get on without him around.

Lee held himself from going through his assault pack. Everything's in there, he thought. Everything's where it's supposed to be.

Being in Ukraine didn't feel strange to Lee. He knew he'd come as soon as the invasion proved real. It also didn't feel strange to be doing it with a battle buddy. He'd trusted someone would answer the bell. It had surprised him, though, that it was Paxton. Everyone he'd expected to say yes, or at least maybe, had balked. Jobs, fatness, families—the typical bullshit, the typical snags. Pax had just been the next name in his phone.

Lee had liked him well enough when they'd served together. Kept to himself, but a good kid, someone you had to show only once what right looked like. Word was he'd had a rough go of it since. Which happened, couldn't fault him for that. But Lee wasn't sure what to make of him now. There was a sullenness Lee didn't recall. And at the airport, when the withdrawal from Afghanistan came up, Paxton hadn't even seemed upset about it, like everything they'd done over there had been for nothing.

"Dumb wars get dumb endings," Pax had said. Then he'd just shrugged.

Lee again set his head against his assault pack. Need to sleep while we can, he thought, closing his eyes. He steadied himself with an old cadence. *I'm not the killer man*, he hummed. *I'm the killer man's son. But I'll do the killing till the killer man comes.*

Pax returned to his window. He pulled out his headphones and plugged them into an old MP3 player. The music of his youth filled his ears. They passed a warning sign for bears. I could've handled that better, he thought. Should've provided half-truths and half-answers, the way you're supposed to. It's what he'd done with the enlistment query. He *had* been a bit of a patriot but he'd learned long ago to never say it out loud. Flag-humping conservatives, clever-mouthed liberals, spoiled-ass civilians, even foreigners like this lady officer, they all glommed onto that word for their own reasons, their own set notions. There was no point in giving anyone that shard of himself ever again.

Boy goes to war to become a man and comes back someone he doesn't know, Pax thought, to a country he doesn't recognize. The biggest cliché on the fucking planet. The least I can do for anyone is keep it to myself.

The bus drove through another checkpoint with barrels of fire and tissue-thin security. "Why are you here?" she'd asked. He could've talked about the legion, how Lee intended to join to get sent to the front, and how he wanted to see if he could do supply work or intelligence or something. Pogue shit, sure, but still soldier shit. Something that helped. It all sounded vague and cloudy in his brain, though, and he knew it'd come out even more so. How to explain to people something he didn't quite comprehend himself? Even if he tried and did his absolute best, there'd be more questions, the kind that sought out detail, the kind that teased out specifics.

It doesn't matter who I am or where I come from, Pax thought. A snarling punk song turned over to a gangsta rap anthem. He began rubbing the beads on his wrist and counting them. I'm here now.

He made it through the beads twice over before stopping. You're lying, he thought, not for the first time since leaving Tulsa. Be honest with yourself, at least. You came because of her and only her and everything else that isn't her is a diversion, and you came because everything has gone wrong and nothing has gone right since the world took her from you.

That wasn't how it had happened, not exactly, but Pax didn't like thinking about that part.

In the notebook in the backpack between Pax's feet was an address scrawled ten years before in cheerful, rounded handwriting. Both the address and the handwriting belonged to a woman named Svitlana Dovbush. Had Pax loved her? Maybe, he thought. No, he thought again—I definitely loved her. I didn't know it then but I did. He'd thought of her intermittently since, sometimes with longing, sometimes with regret, sometimes with a useless fury he didn't know what to do with. It'd been sporadic, though, like summer rain passing through. But I loved her, he thought yet again. Then the invasion of Ukraine happened, and no one anywhere could escape it. Then Pax couldn't stop thinking about Svitlana, and their months together, a torrent of hard memory that beat down and condemned, and then Lee had called, and Pax knew the only choice, the only way to be someone again, was to come here, now, like this. If we could just go back, he kept thinking the night before buying his ticket. To that trip, that weekend, that time. If we could just go back and do it again, we'd get it right.

None of it matters, Pax thought again, looking out the window at more night. I'm here now.

He cycled through the MP3 player, searching. "In the Aeroplane Over the Sea" had been her favorite. He'd liked it well enough but it had been her favorite. He wondered if it still was. The low-fi, acoustic scratching of the song transported him elsewhere.

In the far distance, the shape of a city under cold stars began to emerge. Everything was dark, everything was faint, but it won't always be, Pax thought. Just get to tomorrow. He drifted into a fitful sleep against the glass of the window.

When he woke, the Ukrainian officer was gone. He realized then he'd never gotten her name.

II

_____

The sound of raising blinds wrenched Pax from the pit of
sleep. If he'd been dreaming, he'd already forgotten what
about. Bars of dull gray slanted into the room and across the
mattress on the floor he'd fallen upon in the empty hours before dawn. He'd managed to get his boots off before crawling
into his sleeping bag but little else. The same tee shirt and
jeans he'd put on in Tulsa some forty hours prior now clung
to his skin with dried, tangy sweat. His mouth seemed full of
cotton balls and his thoughts began grappling for regrets it
couldn't quite form, let alone identify.

No, Pax thought. Not one of those mornings. You're jet-
lagged.

"Wakey, wakey, high-speed." Lee stood against the window, eclipsed in silhouette. He stepped forward into the half-light, sure and stout, seeming to smile with his whole body. There was a magnificent cheer about him, as if he'd come here to coach a Little League game. He gripped an extra-large can in his right hand like a mallet and Pax wondered if he'd even bothered to sleep. Lee took a deep, performative swig, a blend of English and Ukrainian script running down the aluminum sides of the energy drink. He wore cargo pants and a black button-down with the sleeves again rolled neatly to the elbows to flash his ink miscellany. They'd called him the Yellow Reb in Afghanistan, to which Lee always had a readymade reply: "Don't get it twisted, I'm from the winning side of the family."

Kinda fucked-up, Pax thought in the apartment flat, looking back on it. They'd been young then. It had been a decade ago. Much had changed. But it's not like I can apologize. That would make things awkward.

He sat up, pulled a flake of dead skin from his bottom lip, and asked what the plan was.

"Meeting in forty with the recruiter." Lee rocked back and forth from the balls of his feet to his toes, his voice cutting, excitable. "There's hot water if you want to shower." Pax had reached the bathroom door when the other man called after him. "Don't drink anything from the sink. Old pipes." He held aloft the aluminum can, his words taking on a cadence of fake reverence. "Courage juice in the fridge—wake up, son! Glory to the motherfucking heroes."

They'd hadn't been in country a day yet, and Lee already had a favorite local phrase.

Pax washed himself in the same rhythmic order he'd learned in basic a dozen years before—hair, pits, arms, and legs, all under two minutes. Then he dressed, a pair of minor accoutrements going on last: a headband to mask his receding hairline, and the prayer beads, wrapped around his wrist like a bracelet. He'd come home from Afghanistan with them and much of their turquoise paint had rubbed off since.

The streets of Lviv were narrow and the Americans pushed down the hills into the city. Both men realized straightaway only dopes greeted strangers here, so they didn't. A dark, nervous energy churned and Pax focused on it so he could avoid the same thing coming from within. He'd taken his duloxetine, with energy drink, of course. So I'll be good, he thought. I'm good. He stopped to retie a boot on a hydrant and an old man with skin of leather stepped around him with something like a vulgarity. Few here seemed to be bothering with masks and hey, Pax thought, what's a pandemic compared to a military invasion? The boundless gray of the sky beat down with gloom, austere imperial buildings and Gothic church domes and pastel houses painted like figurines clashing in sharp, meandering rows. A cultural fault line, Pax thought, repeating to himself a description he'd read in a guidebook on the plane, "Where East meets West." The overhead wire of a passing street tram hissed and sparked and Lee made a joke about dying before Ivan even got to shoot at them, earning an open-eyed stare from a nearby babusya holding grocery bags. Pax saw a little speck of sunlight dancing on a patch of yellow grass. It lay under a bus stop poster of propaganda, a colorful sketch of a Ukrainian badger dismembering a Russian bear in a fur hat, limb by limb. When he looked back the speck was gone.

"Fuck. That's fucking intense," Lee said. He meant the poster. A good amount of cartoon blood covered it. Pax's attention, though, had drifted to a young boy being hustled past them by his mother. He was about seven or eight with curls poking out of a knit cap. He clutched a toy train to his chest and inspected every inch of the strange men speaking foreign words in the fleeting seconds allotted him.

"Hey, dude," Pax said as mother and son turned a corner, "maybe watch the cursing?"

"Eat shit," Lee replied, deadpan. "For one, these people don't speak English. For two, raw profanity is sometimes the only expression of human decency left to us." He smiled. "I'm goddamn transcendent like that."

They passed a casino, the court of appeals, a kebab house, an art gallery. All had been shuttered for the war. The cold began to grip at Pax. He hadn't layered enough under his coat and had skinny desert bones, besides, but it also felt good, in its way. Because it was new, and different from what life had become.

At the bottom of the hill the street lurched into a small square with brown lawns cradled around a fountain of white marble. There was no water and dark moss stains splotched the basin. A pale column shot vertical and on top of it stood a statue of the Virgin Mary, arms out, head ringed by a wreath of lamps. Her eyes cast downward, hollow and damp, and it was hard to tell if she was crying or just refusing to blink. The statue's body had been wrapped and taped in case of shrapnel. Sandbags were stacked against the fountain's base. Lee pulled out his phone and snapped some photographs. Pax thumbed the beads on his wrist and started reciting a prayer out of old habit, first for the bigger stuff, then for himself. He stopped a couple pleas in. What's the point? he thought. You came here, you decided.

Lee nudged him with his shoulder. "Places to be," he said, low. Pax nodded. If the other man registered the many side glances he was getting, he made no notice.

They walked north, up a wide pathway framed by dormant chestnut trees. It was too cold for most people to sit idle on the benches, but one intrepid couple posed for a street artist's rendering. The woman was the right age and had straw, black hair and a hard jawline but it wasn't who Pax sought. A pair of armed soldiers patrolled in front of the KFC restaurant, civilians parting around them like river water around a stone. More armed men, police in flak vests, stood in front of a large pink hotel with four stars etched into its stained-glass windows. Near another monument of black slab, a man in frumpy khakis observed passersby with naked zeal.

"American government or contractor," Lee said. "You can tell by the shoes and watch." And it was true, Pax could see the mighty gleam of both.

The far columns of the opera house guided their way. A minivan was parked across the middle of the path, a big satellite dish swallowing its top. "Shit, fuck," Lee said, then in a whisper, "Stick to me, no English." Only then Pax saw the sign taped to the van's window that read "MEDIA" and all at once a video camera was set on him and a tall woman striding at his side, asking for a few minutes.

"You're here to join the legion, right? You have that look!" She had yellow hair and little, impossibly white teeth. He couldn't help but tongue the backside of his own. The army had fixed his many years before but he'd never stopped being self-conscious about them, still found himself probing along the bottom for the vast gap that was no longer there. He hadn't taken care of them the way he should've. That's on me, he thought. That's on me, like so much else. As he kept walking and the woman kept speaking, about how she didn't have an agenda other than the truth, about how she worked for an unbiased network based in Toronto and wanted the folks back home to know brave men like him had come here to fight for democracy, he thought, a person this striking hasn't spoken to me in a long time. He didn't mean it in a sexual way, more the human-existence kind of way. People from her class and station didn't interact with people like him, not if they could help it. Just how it was. He was trying to figure out how to explain this to her in a way that wasn't aggressive, though now that he thought about it he did sense some of the old hostilities bubbling up, while she spoke so fast and so pleasant and smelled so nicely of jasmine, when Lee paused in front of a kiosk and spun around with sudden violence.

"Salutations, motherfuckers!" He crowed the words, not unlike earlier with the energy drink in the apartment flat. But now his voice held real menace. "We are lost tourists, here on a dirt-cheap vacation package. Could you point us toward Castle Hill? Maybe even spare some coin?" He pantomimed grabbing at the woman's pockets, nothing serious, Pax thought, but enough for her to recoil away and for the cameraman to step between them. Lee was a big man, he had presence. They're not wrong to believe him a threat, Pax thought, watching his friend smile wide for full maniac effect. "Spare some coin!" he repeated. A few awkward seconds followed and then they turned into the crowd, leaving the journalists to their own considerations.

"You're ridiculous," Pax said.

"I'm a goddamn hero," Lee said. "Your knight in shining armor."

Their boots echoed heavy on the cobblestone of the old town. Another Ukrainian child ran by, arms outstretched, pretending to be an airplane. The girl smacked into Pax's side. He bent over and patted her shoulder. Then he said, "Ooga booga." He'd been hoping for a laugh, a visiting Westerner being silly, but instead the kid scurried away with a look of pale terror.

Lee shook his head. "Don't frighten the native youths," he said. "Counterinsurgency 101."

The horizon sat low and smothering, blotted by gray thunderheads. Flurries began to fall scattershot across the day. They stopped at the gate of an Armenian cathedral so Lee could take a photo, then again under a bell tower of an Orthodox church. It's funny, Pax thought, how the older man was drawn to these holy relics but swore if there was a God he'd punch Him in the mouth. Along the church's façade were homemade memorials, dozens and dozens of portraits of young soldiers in uniform, some children's drawings in crayon, too, tributes to dead daddies and uncles, a few mommies and sisters, little flags tucked into corners of the wall, horizontal bands of blue and yellow flickering against the gray.

"Can you imagine?" Pax couldn't help himself. The fallen always turned him a bit maudlin.

"Different than what we did." Whatever register he was on, Lee met him there. "The 'Stan wasn't much of a war but it was the one we got." He put a hand on Pax's shoulder. "Now we get to volunteer for real."

Pax nodded and took a long breath to steady himself but from within he could hear his heart pounding against its cage and he cursed himself for taking only one pill instead of two. Stupid, he thought. Even when you know better you still do stupid shit.

He thumbed his beads and turned to go with Lee down the street. A small group of older kids, teens, maybe, caught his attention. Their secrecy was conspicuous, filing through a spiked, candy-cane-striped gate adjacent to a market. What's that? Pax thought. Let's check out that. But Lee needed him, and he followed.

They stepped into a café. The warmth of the space blitzed Pax's body and then his soul. Dark wood panels and oak tables and chairs gave the café the feel of a forest. Only a couple of tables were occupied by patrons. They walked past them and a fireplace, drafts of tidy heat beckoning and serene.

In a back room they found a man at a table by himself. He looked up and told them to sit. He had arcane blue eyes and strands of white in a sandy beard.

"Welcome to our city," he said, the English jagged but clear. "You may call me Bogdan."

Something about him seemed gaunt, even birdlike. He wore an olive-drab fleece and urban-camo pants, a pistol on his hip, a Makarov, if Pax had to guess. Three cell phones and a batch of manila folders lay across the table, next to an empty espresso cup and a half-eaten pastry. Bogdan asked if they wanted anything to drink. Pax said he was fine. Lee requested water.

"Your papers."

They handed over copies of their DD 214s. Lee went to

explain but there was no need; evidently the Ukrainian had already screened enough American military records to know what did and did not matter.

"Staff Sergeant Han Lee . . . U.S. Army infantry. Honorable discharge. Three combat tours."

"Two to Iraq. One to Afghanistan."

"Check, rog." The soldier lingo popped light off the Ukrainian's tongue. He shifted his focus to the next form. "Corporal Luke Paxton, also U.S. Army infantry . . . general discharge. One combat tour."

"Fifteen months." Pax was surprised at his defensiveness but couldn't help it. It'd been the formative experience of his life. "One fifteen-month tour to the most remote valley of Wardak Province during the height of the surge."

Bogdan's eyes crinkled a bit, and he leaned forward in his chair to size up the visitors. Pax held his shoulders back and met the other man's icy stare, holding his breath. He could feel sweat pooling on his brow and under his pits, it was happening like it always did, and his heart was sounding off again, he could hear it plain as any alarm. They must've been able to hear it, too, how could they not, sitting right there. Stupid, he thought, fucking stupid. Why are you always like this? Then a noise of concession emerged from the local's throat and he reached for the half-eaten pastry.

"I have heard the joke," Bogdan said. "One American army tour counts as three for your air force."

That wasn't the joke but it was close enough. Pax joined the other men in a smile for the moral superiority of the grunt.

"What weapons do you know?"

They replied together. The M4 carbine, of course. The M9 pistol. Claymore mines. They'd both shot AKs in the mountains with Afghan border police, spraying and praying. The M500 shotgun, that was Lee's favorite, no adornment to it, only power. Various light and heavy machine guns, the SAW, for sure, who didn't cherish the SAW, both the M203 and M320 grenade launchers, though the latter was shit, they agreed, the side-loading mechanism didn't work right, it'd been thrust upon them in theater because of big-money Pentagon contracts. The Mark 19, that was Pax's jam, sit behind a belt-fed automatic grenade launcher and let the baby purr. They'd both trained on antitank platforms like the TOW and Javelin but hadn't used them in the 'Stan, there'd been no need. They'd fired 60 mike-mike mortars, 80 mike-mikes, too, and in Iraq, Lee had shot the Four-deuce into an abandoned chemical warehouse. The M107 sniper rifle, though neither had squeezed that particular trigger on an enemy profile, only paper silhouettes. They could call for artillery, still knew the 9-line medevac, direct an attack helo onto target for a gun run. They were infantrymen, paratroopers at that. Weapons were their craft.

"And why are you here?" Bogdan continued, ripping away a bite of food with his teeth. He even eats like a bird, Pax thought. "By choice, you ask for the front. You seek the zero line. This is not normal behavior."

Lee spoke first. "War made my grandparents refugees. If strangers with guns from the other side of the planet hadn't gone to Korea? Shit." Then he sniffed and crossed his arms. "That's what I told my ex-wife and kids. They need to believe I believe that. But maybe I just came here to shoot a Russian invader in the fucking face." A dark relish clambered out of Lee, pervading the table, then the entire back room. "So I can finally look at myself in the mirror and know, fucking *know*, that I'm the killer man."

With that, Lee's body relaxed, shuddering from the remnant energy. He took a drink of water and sat back in his chair. A weird answer, Pax thought, but an honest one.

One of the Ukrainian's phones rumbled on the tabletop. He ignored it. The onus of explanation fell over Pax like a cold shadow.

"I came here," he began, before stopping. Any response he could think of sounded off in his mind, hollow. Lee had told the truth. I should, too, he thought. He tried again. "Well, I came here to help."

The table turned heavy with quiet. He could tell that what he'd said was wrong by the way Lee was looking at him, or not looking at him, more toward him and behind him and around him, but not at him. He couldn't understand, wanting to help is a good thing, he thought, it's why their president has gone on television and asked the world for help, asked combat veterans who'd been in the suck to come and fight. Pax shifted toward Bogdan to say that, to ask who the hell was he to be defying his own leader's command, only to see that the Ukrainian wasn't looking at him, either, but watching something under the table. He followed the other man's craning to his own lap. He was thumbing the prayer beads wrapped around his wrist, not like the lady at the VA had shown him, but manically, hysterically, one-two-three one way, one-two-three-four the other, rinse and repeat, like he was tapping at a video game, like he wasn't bona fide at all but a fraud, a bundle of nerves, a betrayer of the profession of arms itself.

The worst part was, he had no clue how long he'd been going on. Two pills, he thought again, two. You knew it and you still didn't do it. He moved both hands under his thighs and searched for an excuse.

"Old tic," he tried, which was true, in its way, and then Lee tried, as well, saying, "He's high-speed, I'll vouch for him, more than holds his own when the bullets come," but the legion man didn't seem to hear them, instead pushing back his chair and standing with the aid of the table. On the side of his pistol, the right side, he raised his pants to the knee to show his leg, a long metal prosthetic about the width of a broom handle. He knocked against it, twice, as if he was on a neighbor's porch. It pinged low in response. He raised the other pant leg to reveal a second, matching prosthetic. It echoed the same way. Then he returned the bottoms of his pants to position and plucked at a white strand in his beard.

"I've been surprised how many arrivals are willing to fight and kill for my country," Bogdan said, "yet have no idea the war has been going for eight years. Eight years in the Donbas. That's where a land mine got my legs. And I am blessed.

"In old Slavic, Ukraine translates to 'the borderlands.' I tell all my foreigners this because it is important to know the orc mindset. They do not believe we deserve existence, except to provide for them. We are the wheat people who live in the fields beyond, Banderites and dills too simple to appreciate the wonders of the revolution. This isn't like the little American wars you fought in, and I don't mean offense. But those were wars of choice, and you left those countries when the battles ran their course. Here, it's victory or death. We win, or we see Lviv and every other city turned to hell rubble like Mariupol." Bogdan resumed his seat at the table. "What kind of choice is that?"

Pax didn't understand what the Ukrainian was getting at, he hated when people spoke obliquely, the Afghan tribal leaders always did that, so had his fucking boss at AutoHut, for that matter. He'd been raised to say what he meant and mean what he said, both in the army and before it. So he held to the silence. There was authority in the quiet. It forced others to their intentions.

"We were just talking about that outside," Lee said. "Back home we get called volunteers. But it's not true. We were paid. There's health insurance, life insurance, college money. A decent-enough gig if you're not afraid of real work." The dark relish from earlier returned but now it didn't spread from Lee so much as it hovered over him, enveloping him. It was as if he'd been taken up in some bloom, some trance, some creed all its own, and there wasn't any way he was ever coming back from it. "This, though—this is it. Why I wanted to be a soldier in the first place. Something worth fighting for. You know how fucking rare that is? You can take my passport for all I care, Bogdan. I'm here for the long haul. Gimme a rifle squad, point me to the zero line, and we'll rack up skulls for the wheat people."

"Yes." The legion man nodded. "I believe you." Then he ran his fingers through his beard and turned again to Pax.

"The discharge listed on your papers," he said. "Explain this."

Pax couldn't stop himself. He said what he meant and meant what he said, but it was only after saying it—it being "I don't see why that's relevant"—did he realize he'd blown his second shot, the one Lee's vouching had earned him.

One of Bogdan's phones rumbled on the tabletop but he again ignored it. He stuck out his hand for Pax.

"I wish you luck finding a way to help," he said. "My country needs much of it." Then the Ukrainian's avian gaze darted away. He told Lee to be packed and ready, there would be a bus that evening.

"You may be traveling with a group," he said. "Royal marines." He tilted his neck at a hostile angle. "So they say."

Outside it took all Pax had not to purge himself on the cobblestone. He felt dazed and was shaking while trying not to, and kept apologizing to Lee, who had a big plastic smile on his face, saying, "No problem, man, no problem," like they'd just been kicked out of a bar instead of being judged worthy or not.

The weather had turned during their time indoors. A fog had descended, bringing the gray of the sky to earth, and a damp wind now lashed the streets. Flurries still drifted here and there, none seeming to stick. A brittle sort of melancholy had settled over the day and Pax kept thumbing at his beads.

"Ain't no shame in it." Lee had a hand on his shoulder. "Been there myself. Get yourself right, give it another go. I got a contact with a PMC maybe coming over, too . . . Blackwater shit, but the side of good. All that matters."

Then he began going on about how he needed to find a surplus store for supplies, and that Pax could stay in the flat for another two weeks, the donor in the States had prepaid, and Pax understood this was goodbye.

"I'm sorry" was all he could muster.

"Stop that," Lee said, compelling the younger man into a hand slap and one-armed hug. Even through the layers of winter clothing, Pax could feel his physical thrill. "I'll see you out there soon enough. Or not. Do what you need to do, brother. It's on you."

Lee gave him a wad of hundreds, a couple grand in total, American dollars. Pax said he didn't want any charity but the other man insisted. "Can't say the Yellow Reb never hooked you up." Then he was gone, walking away with heavy strides toward the wall of dead soldiers. He turned back, once, raising his fist aloft through the gray.

"Glory to the heroes!" he shouted, loud, guttural, and then he crowed, causing a few passersby to widen their trajectory around him. Despite everything, that made Pax smile.

He wandered the old town without purpose, the cold nursing him. He tried to remember that he hadn't even wanted to fight, not really, not like Lee had. He didn't need it. He was decent at it, or had been, but somewhere along the line he'd become one of those veterans. Washed-up, broken, a man carrying around shards of knowledge that signified nothing and meant anything only to those who'd been there. His own mind had done this to him, not the enemy, not a land mine, but his own consciousness, some defect in his nature. He knew that made it all so much worse. Lee had said there was no shame in it. He'd said that for the obvious reason that there was.

Pax was thirty-three years old and certain his best days were already gone. This had been his chance. Now he had nowhere to go but the tunnels of infernal memory.

He walked and walked. He passed a warehouse of relief supplies. He was handed a flier with the location of a speakeasy operating despite the alcohol ban. He watched more scruffy travelers with their rucks and wondered which ones were real and would serve alongside Lee, and which ones were pretend, like him. He found more walls with portraits of the fallen and a flatcar train saddled with old tanks moving east and saw that this old, medieval city he'd never heard of before coming to it wasn't at war but wasn't at peace, either. More media called at him and he ignored them. He recognized one guy from the coverage of the withdrawal from Afghanistan, he'd been real hysterical about it, and even Pax thought it was crazy his bosses had let him come here so soon after. At the opera house he looked at the winged statues topping it and wanted to know what they represented, but didn't know how to find that out. He thought about asking a stranger to take a photo of him in front of the building, it was the place for something like that, but he got anxious, didn't know who might understand him. So he stood there and stared up at what he decided must be angels and thumbed the beads on his wrist, wishing he could just begin again. I'd do it better, he thought. Or at least different. Then he went to KFC to eat a late lunch.

The fast-food worker didn't know much English, but it proved better than Pax's Ukrainian, and together they managed to order two drumsticks and a side of mashed potatoes. He found a table in the corner and burrowed into the warmth of the restaurant. As he ate, he tried not to think. That's the last thing I should do right now, he thought. Still, when bubbles of American English floated up and over the table partition, he stopped chewing and homed in. Eaves-dropping wasn't a choice so much as an inevitability.

"This is it. Saigon in 'sixty-eight, San Juan in the nineties, Erbil for a spell there." The voice snapped with Midwestern upspeak. "Got here early enough, we'll be able to watch it roll in."

"Like that guy with the connect." This voice was laconic, more neutral. "In Romania."

"Yessir. All shapes and sizes of swinging dicks, coming in hot."

"Like that fucking bar in *Star Wars*."

"More like *Casablanca*." The first voice snickered to itself. "Just need to get the casinos open again."

"Get fucked, cockwaffle." Cockwaffle, Pax thought. Never heard that one before. Lee would love it. "I still need to get you back for that night of hold 'em in Vicenza."

Vicenza! A small grin now touched the corners of Pax's mouth. That was where he and Lee had been stationed, home of the 173rd Airborne. Not many people knew the American army kept an active base of infantrymen in northeastern Italy, sometimes even other soldiers were surprised to learn of it, which meant Pax and these mystery men belonged to the same fraternity. A sense of the fortuitous overwhelmed him.

"Hey," he said, speaking and standing and facing the table

of other Americans in one full rush, "you guys here for the legion?"

He'd believed, and wanted, this other table to be holding a pair of veterans not unlike himself, old enough to not be a babyface in the green machine but still young enough to shoot, move, and communicate on the field of battle. He'd believed, and wanted, them to be fellow travelers, guys here to do the obvious thing with their rucks and stubble and pirate patches. Instead he found two plump men about his dad's age. One had glasses, the other a thick gobbler under his chin. They both wore frumpy khakis and fleece vests, and looked up at him with something between suspicion and ire.

"No," the man with glasses said. "We are not."

"I was in the 173rd," Pax offered. He recognized this would be a short conversation but manners did matter to him. "I heard you all mention Vicenza."

"Yes," the man with the gobbler chin said. "We did."

Only as he returned to his table did Pax see the men's silver watches and polished wing tips.

Out in the cold, Pax made a decision: he needed to leave. He still felt ambivalent about the new money in his pocket but it had given him options. It didn't have to be Tulsa. He could go anywhere to try at something. Svitlana's not here, he thought, there's no way. The smart thing to do with a war is to get away from it, and she was always much smarter than me. Ukraine had nothing for him. He had nothing for it. He'd hoped for it to be otherwise, but hopes were like assholes, everyone had one.

Had Lee told him that? Probably, he thought. It was something Lee would say.

First the flat, he thought. Then another duloxetine. And then—

The witch wail of a siren cut through the city, strident, demanding. Pax hesitated under a naked chestnut tree along the wide pathway while people separated from the crowd piecemeal, some running, others trotting out, all moving with intent.

"Air raid!" a passing voice said to him, and he thought, Oh wow, but also, Am I that obvious?

Most bodies were streaming for a block of stairs that led down to something like an underpass. Pax began hurrying that way, his hands trembling and his skin rising with goose bumps. In Afghanistan they'd controlled the skies, always. This was totally different. What, he thought, could be up there?

He looked and tried to see, but there was only more gray.

Nearing the Virgin Mary again, Pax saw that not everyone had sought cover. Some Ukrainians had made the choice of nothing. A babusya shuffled along the pathway with an unbothered grimness. A group of teens in emo makeup lingered around the monument of black slab, performatively sharing a blunt. And a street artist, the same one he'd seen earlier, sat on a bench, legs crossed, blinking away at the day. She noticed Pax and lifted her sketch pad at him. Despite himself, despite everything, he took a seat on the adjacent bench.

The artist was sallow and gray, sixty or so, wearing a waxed jacket and a black knit cap on her head, half-cocked. Her fingers were covered in tattoos and she said something to Pax he didn't understand. He said, "No," then asked, "English?"

The woman rolled her eyes and said something else he didn't understand. Then she began sketching. Pax focused, as much as he could, on being normal. He took long breaths to steady himself and adjusted his headband for the drawing. He listened to the thump of his heart and the insistence of the siren. Fuck, he thought, looking up at the opaque sky again, what's fucking up there? The artist barked at him, probably with a curse, he thought, and he returned his attention to ground level. What had Lee said about profanity? "Sometimes it's the only expression of human decency left to us."

But fuck, Pax thought again. Nothing about this feels decent. What is up there?

He slid the prayer beads from his wrist and clasped them between his hands, like jewels. The siren kept wailing and he kept rubbing one bead, over and over, feeling its chipped turquoise paint with a fingertip. It calmed him, as he knew it would.

Sometimes, always when he'd been drinking, usually when trying to impress a woman, Pax would say the beads had been a gift from an Afghan child. A boy he'd become friends with, the son of a respected elder, an ally, a man just like him who wanted dignity and purpose and to leave the earth a little bit better than he'd found it. He'd even given the boy a name—Ali—and Ali was a mischievous sort, peddling the Americans DVDs and cigarettes at a markup. He was a good kid, though, a good kid, part of a new generation of Afghans who'd grow up knowing freedom and democracy and all those other fancy words that sound hollow to people who already have them, but mean so much to those who don't.

It was a lie, though, all of it, a figment twisted up by some demented corner of his brain. A harmless one, Pax thought most mornings after, but stupid, something I shouldn't do anymore. Most of the Afghan children his platoon encountered either screamed for chocolate or fled; in the valley over from them, Navy SEALs had wasted some civilians and word had got around. He'd found the beads in the dirt during a patrol through some no-nothing mountain village. Then he'd stuck them in his pocket without bothering to look and see if they might belong to one of the locals watching them from the windows of their mud huts. He'd brought the beads back to the American outpost and cleaned them under canteen water, to have a war trophy, to have something that proved he'd gone and done something exceptional. It was only years later, driving home from a bar through empty dark, that he considered the possibility that someone else, far across the globe, someone who'd watched the act through a window, maybe believed he'd stolen the beads.

And then he maybe believed he had.

The air-raid siren strangled out halfway through its pitch, replaced by the stun of its absence. Pax held his pose for the artist, realizing his internal dread from earlier had been overtaken by a more corporeal dull ache. Which is good, he thought. I can deal with this. People were trickling back to the pathway. As the artist clucked to herself and began erasing something, hard, a shape appeared to his side. It was a girl, brown hair, flat brow, wearing a large man's coat down to her knees, her fingers poking out of rolled-back cuffs like little sausages. Her hair was greasy and matted and she smelled of stale urine.

"Hello," Pax said. She replied in Ukrainian and put out her arms like a plane, lips rumbling to make an engine noise. Only then did he recognize her. She'd bumped into him on the pathway.

"Ooga booga," he tried again, and this time she grinned wide. A set of crooked teeth splayed out, a not-insignificant gap along the top row. Despite her appearance, she carried herself with an air of pomposity. Pax guessed her to be about eleven.

With her head, she gestured toward his clasped hands.

"Wanna see?" He opened his palms so she could view the prayer beads. The girl stepped forward, her tiny eyes not on the beads at all, but pressing on him, looking at Pax in such a way that made him feel like she was staring through him, into all the moral insecurity that growing up in a free country can instill.

Then came the sting of a slap across his face. As he winced, he felt his hands empty.

Holding his jaw, Pax looked up. The child was running away from the bench with a second girl, older, bowlegged, the prayer beads in her grip. They turned at the entry of the old town, on the border between cement and cobblestone.

"Heroyam slava!" the girls shouted, giggling together, then they were gone, spirits lost to the gray.

Pax was standing now, tottering, not from the force of the slap, but from its happening, from his unpreparedness for it. His pulse raced and his breaths became shallow and frenzied. They stole my fucking beads, he thought, realizing he was talking out loud, too. "They stole my fucking beads."

Then he added, "Ali gave me those."

He leaned against the top of the bench, trying to exhale slow, trying not to cry, failing at both. He reached at his wrist for something that wasn't there and that made the whole cycle begin again. It felt like his body might explode and if it could've, he would've let it. A hand was rubbing the center of his back in rhythmic circles and saying something hushed, incomprehensible. He wiped away the blinding tears to find the street artist there.

He managed one clean, deep breath, then another, then said, "Thank you." The artist began walking toward the old town, pattering like a bird. She waved for him to follow. He did.

They entered the cobblestoned maze. The fog was heavy and dense. Though she was only steps to his front, Pax could barely make out the shape of the artist. No one else seemed to be walking these streets, the cold of the coming evening had pushed them inside to fires and companionship. They went left, right, past a registration office for refugees, right, left, through a vacant police checkpoint, left, right, right, along another church's façade with tributes to the dead, left, right, past the café where the justice of the war sat in the back upon his metal legs, right, through an empty market, all the way to the spiked, candy-cane-striped gate.

Trepidation laced Pax's entire being. But he felt something else, too. Something more like thrill.

You came here, he thought. You decided.

He followed the street artist through the gate. He mimicked her exaggerated steps, down a long, dark tunnel, as if they were edging through a minefield. They emerged into a courtyard where there was no fog and it was still day, a childish wonderland unlike anything beyond it. Hundreds of toys filled the courtyard, some old, some new, some soiled from the weather, others store-bought pristine, some placed neatly on bookshelves and cabinets, others bent sideways in the dirt. There were old dolls and theater masks of tragedy and comedy and plush animals and race cars, surrealist paintings of wheat fields put up on the shelves. There were toys galore and Pax wandered the yard, soul glowing. It was one of the most beautiful places he'd ever been, not in spite of its creepiness but because of it, and it felt holy to him. He picked up a muddy teddy bear and set it upright. A group of robot action figures he knew from his childhood were out of order, bad robots mixing with good, so he paused to remedy

that. A rusted-out seesaw that must've been made in the Soviet Union occupied one corner of the yard and he traced the
fulcrum with his fingers. Under the seesaw he picked up a
discarded can of energy drink and read the blend of English
and Ukrainian script on the aluminum. It really was called
Courage Juice, he saw. He'd just assumed that had been another one of Lee's maxims.

A large wooden sign hung from the back wall of the courtyard, a blue-and-yellow flag chalked near it. Pax couldn't
read the sign but someone had drawn out a corresponding
graphic for people like him. One toy was going out of the
yard; another went in. It's an exchange, he realized, not a re-
pository. There were many things he wanted to take, one of
the robots, maybe, the muddy teddy seemed to want a good
home, but he'd brought nothing to offer.

The artist called at him in Ukrainian. He found her among
a mess of shelves. There, at waist level, or a child's eye level,
depending, sat his prayer beads, chipped turquoise paint and
all. The artist clucked at him and he tried not to show his
frustration. He knew what he was supposed to do. But he
didn't know how to do it.

Pax searched his pockets: the key to the flat, Lee's wad of
money, his own passport. That was it. He began unrolling
a hundred-dollar bill—which he figured would more than

cover any toy in the yard, if not all of them—but the artist seemed to scowl. It does feel wrong, somehow, he thought. It wasn't his money. He hadn't done anything for it but failed.

He looked again at the items in his hands. He had no other option. He took his beads, wrapping them around his wrist. Then he placed his passport on the shelf.

The artist tilted her head, narrowing her eyes, as if she were seeing him anew. He handed her a hundred-dollar bill, which she took.

"I'm goddamn transcendent," he said.

Pax left the courtyard, shivering through the cold.

III

"There's a big pie out there, man. A big green pie of tax dollars. And your slice has already been cut. It's just waiting for your skinny jabroni ass to claim it." Lee made a harsh, dismissive sound through his lips. "I'm disgusted. I was one of the noncoms who raised you, and look at this display of abject failure. Goddamn it, Paxton, it's a violation of the code! That money's yours. Get the fucking money."

They were discussing VA disability compensation. Pax had mentioned he'd never filed for any. Didn't feel right, he thought, those funds were for amputees and vets with melted faces. Guys and gals who couldn't get normal jobs back home, like being a mechanic at AutoHut. Those claims were for others, he thought, for those who genuinely needed it. Lee could not tolerate this transgressive inaction.

The older man had returned to the flat late the night prior, awash in disappointment—the alleged royal marines had proven less than authentic, and Bogdan didn't want to waste a chalk to the base on one person. Maybe there'd be one the following day, Bogdan had advised. Stand by.

The two men sat at a table of a barbecue restaurant called the Salo Cave. A rainbow-painted bust of Stalin looked upon them from an adjacent mantel. Everything in the underground restaurant was made from patchwork brick, the walls draped with banners of dead national heroes from history, rebels and scientists and poets and Chernobyl firefighters. Their bowls of blood-red borscht arrived first, each topped with a dollop of sour cream. The waiter winked and handed them two bottles of Putin Huylo beer.

"For our friends from America," he said. "God bless the defenders."

"What's it mean?" Lee asked.

"Putin is Dickhead," the waiter translated.

Everyone laughed. The waiter said he'd be back in a few minutes with their main dishes.

"Here's the real dope." Things were awkward for both of them, Pax thought, they were both in a place between. But they were making the best of it, as they could. "You got a combat record, that's the golden ticket. Auto-qualify for ten percent. Tinnitus, that's what the constant ringing in your head is. When the ear wizard asks, yes indeed, it's constant. Always constant." Lee shook his head like he was explaining something obvious to a child, and continued. "Then you'll do a hearing test. Click the button when there's a ping. All that trigger time and screaming at higher over the radio, you're deaf enough. But during the test, no need to click every time you maybe hear something, you feel me?

"Knees. Back. Shoulders. You were a paratrooper, course there's bone powder in there now. That means more coin. Ain't got a Purple Heart . . ."—Lee had caught a piece of rocket shrapnel in his shoulder in Iraq, a perfect and beautiful six-inch scar he was not above showing off in bars after a few rounds—"but no worries, I don't get as much for that as you'd think." Lee stopped, drumming his fingers on the table for a few seconds, and then sighed. "And that thing you got going on with the shakes and the beads and shit— just being straight with you, brother, that looks like post-traumatic stress to me. Any government shrink will agree. And hey, you earned it. I was in that valley with you, I know you put in the work. They pay for that, too. It's real as the goddamn sun.

"It's all part of the social contract. We put our bodies and lives on the line when no one else would. Fucking civilians pay the tax man so they can ignore what's done in their name. Money goes in, money goes out.

"We're talking like, I don't know, a grand a month. Rent money. Chump change compared to what arms dealers and TV generals haul in. And we actually fucking deserve it. No need to be a noble bitch, Pax. Screws with the system."

With that, Lee sat back in his chair, satisfied. He adjusted the snapback hat on his head at an angle—a cartoon smiley face blared from its crown, alongside the message "Number One Best Grandpa"—and tried his borscht.

"Hearty," he said.

Pax thought about all that while he ate his bowl of soup and drank his beer. If the money has already been allocated for people like me, maybe I should file a claim, he thought. When I get back, whenever that is. He'd come up with a vague notion to travel with Lee's money, to Prague, Barcelona, maybe, someplace he'd never been, a place he could disappear from himself, though planning out how and when was not a wavelength he wanted to explore at the moment. The whole giving-away-of-his-passport complicated matters. And he'd taken three pills in the morning, just in case, numbing him to the day.

That's why Lee gave me all those hundreds, he thought. It's bonus cash. Money he gets for fighting an old war our country authorized so he could come to a new war our country has not, will not, wants very much for us to not be here. Which is wild when you think about it. They're sending Javelins and drones and body armor and surveillance radars, all kinds of weapons, but Lee, he's not supposed to be here, even though he is a weapon, a living, breathing one. So he uses the money he gets for being an old weapon to fund his cause of maintaining himself. It's like the fucking cycle of the military-industrial complex in one body, one person, and the funniest thing is, he hates the military-industrial complex, calls them leeches.

It was all too much. "Gonna hit the latrine," Pax said.

The extra duloxetine mixed with the alcohol was making him feel a bit loopy. On the way to the bathroom he walked past displays of old machine guns on tripods, stacks of portable radio transceivers from World War II, and the husks of spent howitzer shells. This is what the Google reviews mean by "Nationalist theme," Pax thought. He took a shit and wiped his ass with toilet paper imprinted with Putin's face, then washed his hands and returned to their table.

Lunch had arrived, pig ear and snout for Lee, pickled herring for Pax, a plate of dumplings for them to share. Lee asked about a second round of beers, but the waiter shook his head.

"The ban," he said, as if that explained both the first round and the vetoed second.

Lee was beginning negotiation attempts when a voice boomed across the restaurant with hail-fellow-well-met authority: "Staff Sergeant Lee! Corporal Paxton! What are you two fine sky soldiers doing here?"

Something about the voice, its timbre, the way it inflected, disturbed Pax. It didn't so much penetrate his pharmaceutical calm as much as bludgeon it, a sledgehammer through stone. The little hairs on the back of his neck rose. His empty gut growled into the beyond and his lizard brain began telling him, run, run now, but his body did not oblige, he was fixed to this meal, and this table, and this chair. He watched as recognition came over Lee, and it wasn't bitter, like it should have been, but cordial, even warm. This inspired true fury in Pax. Because you should know better, he thought of Lee. You of all people should know. Then Captain Jordan Todd "J.T." Merriman Jr., U.S. Army, infantry, commanding, stood at their table, grinning out at all the world like they were old pals.

"Hey, sir." Lee was smiling now, too, standing, shaking hands with the enemy. "Been a minute."

"Ten years, can you believe it!" Merriman was tall and lean, mannered in a natural way. He'd come to their unit in Afghanistan midtour as the new commander, replacing a burnt-out one. He'd stayed long enough to bring them back to Vicenza. Most of them, anyhow. There had been that unfortunate business at the checkpoint, Pax remembered, not that he could forget, and he'd tried to. That's why Lee's smiling, he thought. He hadn't been there. Anyone who wasn't there could never understand how it went as it did, but Pax had been. So he kept to his chair and crossed his arms, listening to their former captain ask about Lee's life and Lee's family with his officer mouth and his officer words, like he gave a singular fuck.

"And young Pax." Merriman put out his hand. Despite himself, Pax reached up and took it, feeling the inevitable palm crunch and power tilt. "How have you been getting along?"

"Doing fine," Pax said. Then he lied again. "Good to see you."

He was surprised to find the decade had aged Merriman as it had. The man's tawny skin had splotches in it, and streaks of gray ran rampant through his thinning dark hair. Black, rectangular frames, hipster glasses, Pax thought, covered his face, still so angular, still so patrician. And yes, there it was, the eternal certainty, but Pax had seen what it looked like when that confidence shattered, and he remembered as he stared back, hard, until the other man glanced away.

"How's life on the inside?" Lee asked, leaving out the compelling part: no active-duty servicemembers were supposed to still be in Ukraine.

"Got out a couple years back." Another surprise. Captain Merriman had exuded pure lifer while in command, the sort of careerist who'd quote field manuals and regulations to the letter, and then cite some ancient Greek battle as a case study to cherry privates who'd barely gotten through high school. He wasn't a West Pointer but something even worse: a Stanford grad who thought his years of "regular" college had instilled in him some ethereal, interpersonal touch with the common folk. "Big change but I've figured it out."

"How ever did the green machine go on," Pax said.

No one responded to that. Merriman went on to explain that he'd become a consultant, whatever that meant. Lee asked if he was in-country for business or pleasure.

"Yes," Merriman said. He craned out his neck. "Tell me you're not here for what I think you are."

"You know it!" Lee beamed. "Gonna get my slay on, sir. Wanna come?"

Merriman offered a cursory smirk but then said, "Be careful. Everything I've heard about the legion is that it's sloppy.

Good intentions, poor execution. I have a contact with the Georgians—they accept foreign volunteers, as well, and already have the structure in place."

Lee waved that away. "I know what I'm doing," he said, which struck Pax as off. He knew as much as the other man did about the legion, which was next to nothing. He held to the quiet, though. He was his brother's keeper.

"Well. Here's my contact info in case you need a rip cord. This is my standard line, this one's encrypted." Merriman typed the numbers into Lee's phone, then looked up. "You, too, Pax? Here to volunteer?"

It was such a simple question but Pax wasn't sure how to answer it. He saw Lee leaning forward to intervene. Then a warm glow swelled from within. What does it matter? he thought.

"I came to help," Pax said. "But I don't know how."

"Hmm." Merriman raised his fingers to his lips; they were long and sleek like tongs. They'd joked in Afghanistan that Captain Merriman called himself Colonel Merriman when he looked in the mirror, every line unit had an officer with ambitions like that, he'd been theirs, and as he stood there in a barbecue restaurant in Lviv, Ukraine, Pax wondered what brigade in Uncle Sam's army had been spared his leadership because of that unfortunate business at the checkpoint.

"There's a program starting up—well, there's a couple of them, but the one I'm thinking of involves local civilians," Merriman continued. "Teachers, doctors, bus drivers, people who want to learn basic combat skills. Under the umbrella of territorial defense, but more informal, more like an armed neighborhood watch. Give these people a shot at survival if the ground invasion comes this way. They're looking for more trainers. You have the résumé, for sure. Want me to pass along your name?"

It sounded amazing. Pax knew in his bones this was the kind of thing he could do, he would thrive at, he could find real purpose in. Training was teaching and teaching was just meeting people at their level and bringing them to yours. He'd done it as a corporal, he'd done it as a mechanic, and he was good at it, he was a good and practical and hands-on teacher. Even Lee looked approving. But then there was the way their former captain was standing, his popsicle-stick posture. And his big straight teeth, his officer words and officer mouth. And his stupid fucking hipster glasses, and that eternal conviction, acting like everything between them was fine and that nothing at the checkpoint had ever happened. But it had. It all made Pax recoil.

"Naw," he said. "I'm cool."

"Well. Keep me apprised on things." Merriman didn't

seem bothered by Pax's rejection. It was as if the idea about the training had just been a way to get through the conversation. His eyes sparkled behind his lenses as they found the bust of rainbow Stalin. "Hey, let's get a group photo with that. What a crazy place to run into you guys!"

Pax scanned the restaurant. It's not crazy, he thought. He saw tables and tables of young and middle-aged men with rough stubble, wearing tactical-chic clothing, eating bowls of borscht and drinking their one allotted Putin beer, studying him as he studied them. It's not crazy at all. Other than the staff, most everyone in the Salo Cave looked a lot like them.

———

Merriman watched the two depart, Lee the sauntering lead, Paxton hunching along in his trail. Odd, he thought, how everyone settled into their old roles with such ease. He'd once begrudged his commander self, finding it grating, excessive in its optimism and confidence, but that was the gig, the job. Soldiers required presence from their leadership. He'd needed to give them such a man.

It'd been years since he'd allowed himself to be that way. It felt nice, Merriman admitted. Still fits, like an old sweater.

The military allowed for leaders to put people first. His profession now did not. Just how it was.

It'd been good to see Lee. A classic American noncom, through and through. The sort of ground leader who separates us from the Russian mil. Paxton, though. He'd always been a brooder, the type of soldier who loved to gripe about the decision-making but got quizzical when presented the opportunity himself. Held his own during firefights, which mattered, but turned dizzy when he had too much time to sit around and think.

Be generous, Merriman told himself. Last he'd heard, Corporal Paxton had found life on the outside difficult.

Still—what did he have to complain about? An entire squad had been at that checkpoint. Paxton was the only one who'd walked away unscathed. The shrapnel remaining in Merriman's hip proved it. Six wounded, one killed, and Paxton, sheltered in, and saved by, the gunner's cupola.

Those numbers didn't even include the body count of locals. Merriman had overseen the cleanup. Limbs paired with the wrong bodies. Intestine bits dangling from trees. A child turned to pink mist her grandmother kept trying to wail back to existence. Etcetera.

He reached for his encrypted phone and cycled through the contacts. He knew the team tasked with keeping track of citizens in-country. Merriman somehow doubted either of his former soldiers had bothered to register with the embassy.

———————

Bogdan texted. It was time. Pax and Lee lingered outside the restaurant. It wasn't quite cold enough to blow an air ring and see it but Lee still tried.

"Why the animosity?" he asked. "We went to war with that man."

Embers of Pax's fury remained. "What kind of grown-ass adult uses initials as his first name?" he said. "It's dumb."

"Come on. For real."

You don't know? Pax thought. He couldn't believe the other man. But it was goodbye, again, and he didn't want to spoil things.

"Always took him as a rich kid there for his own reasons. Stanford this, Ranger School that." He thought, yet again, of the checkpoint. "Not willing to get his hands dirty but expected others to."

"Wasn't the best commander I had." Lee shrugged. "Far from the worst. I'm telling you, I'll take the guy who knows he's an officer over the one playing bang-bang cowboy, trying to be one of the boys." He spat onto the ground. "They get people killed."

"No," Pax said. He couldn't help himself. "The other kind does, too."

Lee pursed his lips and knocked at his own forehead, seeming to rack his mind. "That was him? The checkpoint?"

"The checkpoint."

"What was that kid's name?"

"Shiloh. Private First Class Shiloh." Pax couldn't remember the first name. Neither he nor Lee had known him very well. No one had. He'd been a cherry in-country with them less than three weeks. Pax had helped scoop up the remains, called him his brother in arms, shed tears when he packed the personal effects to send home to the family, but now he couldn't even summon the boy's given name he'd gone by for all the short nineteen years he'd walked the planet.

Fucking remember, Pax thought. What's wrong with me. It's my duty to remember.

"Messy shit, man. Messy shit." What did Lee care? He hadn't even known Merriman had been there, been in charge that bleary day. "Gotta let it go. Otherwise it'll eat you up from inside, and the enemy gets another tally."

"Terrance!" Pax shouted the name, raising it from some fathom of derelict memory. "His name was Terrance."

Lee nodded. "That's right," he said. "Had him on a memorial bracelet. Nine names on that sucker. No." He sniffed. "Ten."

They decided not to jinx the farewell this time. They exchanged a hand slap and one-armed hug and Pax said it before Lee could: "Glory to the motherfucking heroes."

"You know it, son. You know it."

Pax was alone again. But today he'd managed a plan. A guise of one, at least, complete with a translated map and phrase book he'd found in a drawer in the flat. He'd thought about it all night. There's no chance, he reminded himself. And when I confirm Svitlana's not here, it's on to Barcelona.

Pax had never lived in one place a full decade. Why would anyone else?

Bright air hovered through the afternoon. Patches of sun scattered the avenues and the cold's grip lessened with every minute and every step. The fairy tale of old town with its castles and palaces and litany of churches seemed less impenetrable now, because now he had a map, and because of the map he could identify and catalog. That wasn't a square but Rynok Square. That wasn't any cathedral on a hill but St. George's Cathedral on a hill. That bell tower belonged to the Greek Catholics and those stained-glass windows belonged to the Roman Catholics, and that architecture style was Renaissance and that one Baroque, and that mosaic wasn't just old but goddamn fourteenth-century old. These details mattered to Pax. They gave him bearings. They grounded and included him.

He saw unflattering artwork of Putin on every block: Putin with a Hitler mustache, Putin with bloody-red handprints smeared over his likeness, Putin sucking a dick. A young person of indeterminate gender walked by wearing a sweatshirt of the Madonna cradling a rocket launcher. "Saint Javelin the Protector," the shirt read. He stopped to admire another bus-stop poster: a human form prostrate on the ground, a sunflower sprouting from its chest. He pulled out his phrase book and pieced together the message underneath: "Occupiers make the best fertilizer."

He thumbed his beads. In Wardak the locals had farmed apples and opium.

The sound of church bells greeted Pax as he entered an unmarked square. It was discreet and quiet, some sort of service starting up in the little Gothic chapel across the way. The figure of the steeple cleaved the square down the middle, half in sunlight, half in shadow. Small groups of soldiers milled about, armed with AK-74s, the laminated-wood stocks and handguards gleaming with stockroom polish. They'd inserted their rifle magazines, Pax noticed, though that didn't necessarily mean they'd chambered a round. All depended on the threat index.

A bronze statue drew him to the center of the square. It was a monk, up to Pax's sternum, with a tonsured scalp and a shit-eating grin. The reason for this lay upon the monk's shoulder, a barrel of beer hunted-and-gathered to aid monastery worship. A clock sat in the barrel's face. When Pax moved the arrows to reflect the proper time, he heard a spring cranking inside the barrel, and then the arrows returned back as they'd been. This clock could not be broken. For the monk, it seemed it would always be five o'clock.

On a restaurant patio, two men wearing rubber dishwashing gloves were pushing cloths deep into the mouths of open wine bottles. Another was funneling a dark liquid into other bottles, ethanol or gasoline, Pax thought, they're making Molotov cocktails, here, out in the open. Against the foundation of an apartment building, two teens nuzzled and cooed to one another. Nearer, on a bench, a woman in a cocked knit cap fed bread crumbs to loud, ornery birds the shade of midnight blue. It wasn't the street artist from the day before but Pax walked close to check.

He found another bench under brittle winter trees and pulled out the map. He was two streets over from the tram.

One of the birds began squawking at him. Its belly and flanks were clear white and its tail held a dark, metallic gloss. Its plumage seemed soft and dense and it remained in place, squawking, even when Pax air-kicked at it.

"Go away, bird," Pax said. It was a crow, he thought, some

Eastern European magpie thing and it would not shut up. Its eyes were velvet-black and relentless and it didn't stop cawing until he rose from the bench and walked at it. Then it glided around him, assuming its perch on the bench he'd just vacated.

The bird cawed again.

Which one of these high-speeds will let me borrow their AK, he thought, looking around the square. Won't need it long. He glimpsed a familiar face in a window front. The chubby, bemused visage of the world's richest man tumbled out. He moved to it, away from the bird. A framed photograph had been elevated upon a stack of books, a half-moon of scented candles surrounding it as a shrine.

"Elon, maximum cool!" A man stood in the store's doorway, watching the day. Or leering at the teens fondling each other, Pax wasn't sure. He wore a coyote-brown fleece with a patch on his shoulder. He was burly, head and face freshly shaved, eyebrows freshly plucked. Above him, a flag with a black sun drooped against the flat wind.

Pax asked if he spoke English.

"Tiny English."

"Why's he maximum cool?"

"Starlink!" The man tapped the Velcro patch on his shoulder. It displayed the silhouette of a dog, a shepherd with pointy ears and bared teeth. "Azovstal!"

Pax pulled out the phrase book again. Through some trial and error, he learned that this man's dog unit had been fighting in the underground tunnels of the abandoned steel plant in Mariupol. Starlink was a satellite system owned by Elon Musk, and the only way the holdouts were able to communicate with their command and families.

"How will they get out?" Pax asked.

The man's broad nostrils flared and he clenched his fist. "No leave. Fight to all death."

A heavy pall fell over them. The man was shaking with emotion, red-faced and intense, and Pax put his hand on his shoulder. "That's some Alamo stuff," he said. "Respect." Church bells from across the square rang again. The man said something in Ukrainian, and when Pax grunted in incomprehension, he seized the phrase book and turned its pages himself.

He found a word and pointed to it. "National." The man turned some more pages then pointed again. "Idea."

Something's off here, Pax thought. Though he wasn't firm on what. "Got a thing," he told the man. "See you around." But he had to wait to cross the square. A long, shiny hearse was pulling around it, moving at a crawl. A collection of mourning Ukrainians in suits and veils now occupied the chapel's steps, some loud with their grief, others withholding it. The soldiers in the square began to gather. They were to carry the casket inside. A black ribbon dangled from the hearse's rearview mirror. As it passed, the man with the dog patch snapped to attention and saluted.

Mykhaylivskyy Street, 7A
L'viv, L'vivs'ka oblast, Ukraine
79000

The address was seared into Pax's mind he'd looked at it so many times, yet he still pulled out the notebook from his backpack to verify. He took tram 10 to Shevchenko Grove, then transferred to tram 7.

He sat by himself thinking about the dead Ukrainian soldier from the square. He felt certain that somewhere in the country there was a Ukrainian captain responsible, and somewhere else there was another Ukrainian soldier who could've stopped it but didn't because he'd been ordered not to. They didn't have car bombs here, he knew that, it wasn't that type of war. But whatever the equivalent was had taken that man.

And it'll be the other soldier, Pax thought, not the captain, who's trapped in the amber of those failed seconds until he dies or kills himself or drinks it all away. It wasn't fair but what could you do. It was the same everywhere. War snatched good and not-good alike, the tender and the fierce, those who deserved it and those who didn't, those who chose to pick up a weapon and fight and especially those who didn't want anything to do with it at all. This was known, this was belabored. War was as simple as it was inevitable. That's what allowed such clean pronouncements on it. What was less known, Pax thought, looking out the window of the street tram, was how it baited those who survived it, seduced them, deluded them, trailing them like an old loyal dog until of course you turned around and said, Come on, boy. Some missed and longed for it, nostalgia is such a sanitized dream, others raged for what it genuinely took and what they needed to pretend it did. But the force of it all. That's what Pax had been feeling again since crossing the border. The absoluteness of war's force. Pax was a nobody, a has-been, a never-was, a man far from home. Of course I can't escape it, he thought, but even that's a dodge because I came here, same as Lee, same as them all, the gobbler chins and the battle freaks and the lost souls and even goddamn fucking Merriman. You came here, you decided. Any accord with what happened before was never a choice, not a real one, anyway, not for him. Yet here he was. And the other peace, the big one, it's no wonder it never lasts. Peace was inaction and war was action and basic physics answered this long ago so I just need to stop thinking and shut up, he thought.

He got off the tram at the stop for the cemetery. He walked north, along its western fence line, watching more midnight-blue birds watch him. He knew seeing that she didn't live here anymore would do something for him. He didn't know what but it would be something. Fuzzy images of Barcelona, or what he pictured Barcelona being, flitted through his mind. Dancing women. A tranquil sea. Warm conversations with strangers who knew nothing of what he was or who he'd been. He fingered the wad of money in his pocket and thought how lucky he was to have a friend like Lee.

The cemetery's edge ended and a neighborhood began. Gray high-rises dotted the horizon but most of the buildings in his immediacy were a creamy orange. Chipped paint splotched many of the sides, revealing sunburnt brick.

In this part of the city, neither the season nor the war seemed an excuse for botanical sloppiness; tidy winter gardens pocketed the front of each of the buildings. Pax stopped at a bed of little tulips trying to emerge. The street was empty of other people but he could hear electronic music rumbling from some upper floor behind him. A cranky air vent moaned nearby. A sign next to a metal gate carried the marking "7A" and behind the gate was a child's scooter and above the scooter was a windowsill and in the windowsill sat a striped cat, lounging in the sun. The wall-mounted mailbox had a name. "Chernenko," it read.

See, Pax thought, not her. Svitlana disliked cats, for one. Never wanted kids, for another. And it was impossible for him to imagine the party girl he'd known on her hands and knees tilling flower-bed dirt, even as the thought of it brought a wry smile to his face. Svitlana had been many things. A keeper of a home garden was not one.

I Came, I Saw, I Walked Away, he thought, doing just that. He made it four steps before pausing. Chernenko, he thought again. Had that been the name of that guy? It'd been so long, Pax had seen it only once, when he'd hacked into her Facebook and pulled up her private messages and copied-and-pasted them into Google translate, and learned what she thought about him and them, or what she told this person about him and them, some girlhood crush she'd been corresponding with because she was lonely in Vicenza living around so many foreigners who knew nothing of her and nothing of Ukraine and didn't even bother trying to, she was just another gap-year wanderer from Eastern Europe passing through, and there's no way, he thought again, Chernenko,

Chmilenko, Potapenko, the names all sound the same, and now you're being racist on top of being paranoid and you need to walk away.

He didn't, though. He stood there thinking, trying to remember. He didn't know how long he stood there, but it proved long enough for a person in a hurry to close and lock the front door to 7A and approach the metal gate. It was a woman with straw, black hair and a hard jawline. At first she seemed annoyed that someone lingered on the street. Then she became perplexed.

"Luke?"

It was her. It was Svitlana. The feeling in his chest swelled again. He heard himself exhaling and then words came from his throat.

"Hello," he said, then tried again. "Hey, Gypsy."

She seemed to scowl at the old pet name, but then she was there, through the metal gate, clasping his forearms and pecking his cheek with her lips. He felt the steam of her breath on his face. She stood about as tall as him with her straw, black hair and her hard jawline that seemed to have rounded out some in the years between. He smelled traces of her shampoo as she stepped back, coconut, he thought, watching the olives in her eyes quiver.

"I like your flowers," he said.

"They came up too early." She groaned. Then she asked what everyone seemed to want to know. "Why are you here?"

He couldn't get it out. He wanted to say, "For you," "To see you," "To help you," but he didn't know which version to offer, so instead he used Lee's joke.

"Cheap vacation package. Couldn't say no."

She smiled. He'd always been able to make her laugh. It was how they'd met. Everyone else grinding on each other's bodies on the dance floor while they sought out a corner, him figuring out ways to make her laugh, her waiting him out until he did. She hadn't been one to laugh at soldiers' jokes just because, and he'd recognized that. It'd made the pursuit of them all the more worthwhile.

Long time ago, he remembered. He steadied himself.

"I came to help. With the war. I don't know. Not to fight. Something else. Was in the area. And here you are."

"Here I am." Her straw hair was parted in the middle and fell to her neck and she wore a bulky jacket that framed a solid build. Linebacker shoulders, he remembered, he used to tease her about them, and then he'd had to explain what linebackers were. Leather gloves hid her hands but he knew bright, vibrant nails lay under there, it was her thing, something she took great pride and care in. A pair of simple brass tridents fell from her ears, and Pax knew there was a matching version inked across her right hip, much larger. He remembered running his lips and tongue over the tattoo in hotel rooms across Italy, stealing away with her for weekends and holiday leaves to Florence, Cinque Terre, Sardinia, Jesolo, because they'd been young then, and free, with a little bit of money and a singular interest in discovering themselves together.

"How—how did you find me?"

"Oh." He held up the notebook. "Don't suppose you recall writing this down for me. In, umm, Milan."

Pax sensed a tautness in the air. He didn't like it. Svitlana raised the hood of her jacket. "Luke, I'm sorry," she said, "but I must go pick up my son from his swim lesson."

Swim lessons, he thought. There's a war on and you're talking about swim lessons?

"Definitely. Apologies." He took a step back into the street to give her clearance. She has a son, he thought. Of course she has a son. It's been ten years. People have sons. "Nice seeing you, Lana."

She smiled with her lips closed, nodding as she passed, and he was watching her back for seconds that felt like pangs, then she turned around and said, "I don't know what your plans are, but—"

Yes, yes, of course, yes, he was thinking, and she was still talking, something about a dinner with friends the following evening, all you ever had to do was ask, and when she finished, he breathed and stood up straight against the day and thought, Thank You, I don't know if You're up there but if You are, thank You, I owe You, thank You.

"See you then."

"See you."

IV

He stood in front of a steel sliding gate that led to a house on a hill, certain this was the right place. Through the dusk Pax could see the three-storied stone home with a high, hipped roof and oval gable windows that suggested a welcome the gate refuted. The house popped with Tuscan-yellow verve, the windows trimmed white, a small wooden balcony with an overhang jutting out from its side like a broken tooth. There was no one on it, though; no one seemed to be anywhere. Pax checked the address on his phone and looked again for something like a doorbell or knocker.

"Hello," he said to the house, to the air, to the falling sun, to anything that might hear him. He gripped a bouquet of sunflowers and tugged at the collar of his new dress shirt and began to shout, "My name's Luke, hello! I'm with Svitlana."

She'd texted the dinner details that afternoon, along with an admonition: "Please don't call me (or anyone!) Gypsy here. It's considered offensive. See you tonight."

He'd known it was offensive, it's why he'd called her that, to tease her, to show her she was special to him. But things had changed, and he didn't mean only the world's sensibilities. She has a son now, he reminded himself. She's a mother. There can be gypsy mothers but not mothers called Gypsy and please for the love of Christ stop thinking.

The low rumble of the gate saved him from himself. He waited for it to slide past, then began the slow march up the hill. Two cars were parked on the slope, both Mercedes SUVs, and Pax told himself to admire the cars for what they were, elegant machines, nothing else or more. Your hang-ups are your own, he thought. You are a guest. Behind him, toward the city center, came the peal of church bells.

A stout, chipper woman with auburn hair greeted him at the front door. "Welcome," she said. "I am Yeva and I am pleased to have you." Her English was dense, a tangle compared to Svitlana's, and she slowed it down when Pax tilted his head. "These are beautiful, thank you. Svita, Mister Graves has come!"

Pax didn't know what that meant and didn't have time to ask. The hostess took his coat, then seized him by the elbow and escorted him—delivered, really—to a wide octagon space brimming with artificial light. Clumps of people stood around couches and chairs as if they were decorations, and dozens of eyeballs splatted onto him at once. From an unseen loudspeaker wafted the melody of a horn solo.

He breathed through his nostrils and thumbed his prayer beads and thought, You're good, man, you're good, and he said, "Is that jazz?"

Then he was surrounded, hands thrust into his, strange faces wagging and watching and smiling in that taut, stern way he'd learned was the Ukrainian manner. He heard a voice saying, "Siri, volume down, Siri, volume down." Another was talking about an international jazz festival hosted in Lviv. Yet another said he thought Americans weren't supposed to bring flowers but Javelins. And still another voice, the most forceful one, was asking if he preferred vodka or cherry liqueur.

"It's a flavored brandy, local. You'll love it." Pax sought out the clear American cadence with a dog's hunger. A short man who stood tall cleaved through the group to introduce himself. He had silver hair and a cubed jaw and he winked when Pax found his face. "Fear not, you're not the only yankee here."

"Oh wow," Pax said. "You're the guy from the news." He was the man Pax had observed a couple days prior in the old town, the one who'd gone hysterical during the withdrawal from Afghanistan yet was here, in Ukraine, six months later, covering a new war. "Derek Mercer."

"Indeed." Derek Mercer said this with a knowing sense of irony, just enough to make it seem like he was in on the joke, that he too believed the whole business of being a public figure was a silly game brought on by happenstance. Yet the world's stories needed telling. "I hear you're a combat veteran. Thank you for your service, son."

Pax never knew what to say to that so he tried out, "Sure thing," which also didn't work. More introductions were made. A prim man about Pax's age said he was Yeva's older brother despite being half her size. A gangly Lviv native called himself a volunteer, and insisted on as much English as possible this evening. "Only way to improve," he said. A pretty woman wearing blush said in a singsongy accent she was an aid worker from the Netherlands. She in turn introduced a Latvian food driver who just nodded at Pax, and a wizened woman from the UN who didn't even do that. A judge from Kyiv was referred to as the Judge. Yeva's younger brother, a round, bespectacled man in his early twenties, sidled up last, wearing a wrinkled button-up and pajama bottoms.

"Roman Boyko," he said, demanding a fist bump instead of a handshake. "We are allies tonight in the danger zone."

Pax pondered that. "Are you quoting *Top Gun*?"

Roman's face stretched out in a reptilian grin. "The further on the edge," he said, "the hotter the intensity."

There were more than a dozen people in the room. Svitlana was not among them. Pax watched the aid workers move away from him and he figured it was because he was American, or a soldier, or both. A third group also hung back: an old man with crooked shoulders deep in the folds of an armchair, a woman at his side with stark white hair, and a bushy, middle-aged man who must've been six and a half feet tall.

"Our parents," Roman said. "Proud, noble Ukrainians who won't understand a thing you say. My dad will smile at you for it. My mother will glare."

"And the big dude?"

"Found him on the road between Crimea and Kherson last year," Andrei, the volunteer, said. "He's been with us since. He says little but works like a horse. He wears his beard like a Tatar but if he is one, that is only a guess. So we call him—" Andrei paused to ask Roman for the translated word.

"Unknown."

Pax watched Unknown sip a glass of water with knuckles the size of a shovel. The man was gazing out a half-shuttered window, where the muddy light of the dying day was puddling, pretending to listen to the old couple. Wherever he was mentally, Pax thought, it was far from this cocktail party.

Pax's cherry brandy arrived. He clinked glasses with Yeva and the others.

"Slava Ukraini," they said.

"Slava Ukraini," he repeated, taking a healthy swig from his glass. It was cool and sweet in his mouth and burned a bit down his throat, enough to keep it from tasting like children's juice.

"Where's Svitlana?" he asked. He'd come here for her, to see her, not be a hapless foreigner for the local upper-middle class.

"She's upstairs and will join soon," Yeva said from somewhere behind him. "Her husband called," someone else said, and his stomach hadn't finished dropping when Roman said, "Former husband," and then his sister was shushing at him while Roman continued, "What? It's true, you always yell at me for saying true things."

Pax turned to the clever young man wearing the mask of a fool and considered his options. He spoke low, through his teeth.

"Please explain."

"Whoops." Roman laughed to himself. "Right. Here's what I know, my new friend. They were divorcing. Long process in

Ukraine when a child's involved. And Chernenko's one of the best defense attorneys in the city, comes from an old Galician family, very powerful. He was not making things easy. Then the war comes. Our lawyer-hero goes off with the Lviv reserve unit to do the vital duty of sleeping in mud and boiling Russian teenagers in tanks. Now Svita, poor Svita, good patriot that she is, must wait for him." He pulled out an electronic cigarette, taking a long drag of some sweet-smelling vapor. "You see, we are not as progressive a country as we could be. I have traveled Western Europe, Portugal, Ibiza. And France! Now that's a land to be experienced. I met this brunette there, the places she could reach with her tongue—"

"Durnyy!" Yeva ended her brother's pontifications, striding over and trying to snatch the vaping tool from his lips. "Vyrodok!" Roman shielded himself by holding up his arm like a wing, laughing and coughing in chorus. Pax didn't care about any of it. Husband, he thought. That's bad. Divorce, though. That's good. A divorce on pause? He wasn't sure what to make of that. He sipped his cherry brandy as Roman used him as a human buffer. Yeva reached over his shoulder and smacked her brother. Pax tugged again at the collar of his new dress shirt. My neck got fat, he thought. How does a neck even do that? Yeva reached over again and smacked her brother again.

Married a fucking lawyer. He could feel sweat pooling under his arms. I should've taken two, he thought.

Roman excused himself to go vape on the balcony. Pax talked with Yeva for a few minutes, not about Svitlana or marriage or divorce but about the house, and how the house was a manor, and how the neighborhood had been built a century back for Polish military officers. He had difficulty penetrating her accent still but they managed. He asked what she'd called her brother, and she translated, helping him practice a couple times himself. "Dur-nyy!" "Vyr-o-dok!" Next he mingled with Olek, the family's eldest son, an architect for the city who said he'd been keeping busy with temporary housing for displaced easterners. Olek wore an embroidered, collared shirt with blue-on-white stitching, little sundials sewn into it. It was the same pattern, Pax saw now, that the Boyko patriarch wore on his dress shirt across the room.

"There are differences, yes. Language. Cultural. Economic, sometimes." Up close, Pax saw how much Olek resembled his siblings; he was slighter, but shared the same strong chin and wide-set eyes. "But this is a way to show what we have in common. This is the vatniks' mistake." Olek tapped at his chest. "What better way to make us unite? If we were not a real nation before, we are now."

"I saw similar in Afghanistan," Pax said. He couldn't help himself. It'd been the place that taught him how the world worked. "Nothing brought opposing groups together like we did."

"That must've been hard to watch." The Ukrainian's voice softened. "The exit."

"Yeah." Pax hadn't been surprised by the mess of the withdrawal but he had been surprised at the sting it'd come with. "I don't know." Not that his personal bitches mattered in the face of mass tragedy. "I guess dumb wars get dumb endings."

"An unforced error. A colossal one." Derek Mercer joined them. He'd grabbed a bottle of cherry liqueur and topped off their glasses. "A stain on America's honor."

"So what," Pax said. "How about all the dead soldiers, all the killed civilians?"

"Yes." The newsman seemed startled, even confused. "We're in agreement. That's exactly what I mean."

It didn't feel like they agreed but Pax began counting out invisible beads in his head and held to silence. Olek tended the gap, asking Derek Mercer what he expected to cover while in Ukraine.

"A fine question. I've seen much as a correspondent. Disfigured orphans. Shattered widows. Men cut down in the prime of their life because they took one step in the wrong direction." He paused to sniff at the absurd ruin. "We may go to Kharkiv and stand in line with those waiting for frozen chicken legs and hot soup. That's something people need to see. I met a veteran fresh from the front yesterday whose pupils cover his entire eyes. That's a man I'd like to get on camera. The owner of your area soccer club has turned his field into a tent city for refugees, and—"

"Displaced," Olek said. "Not refugees. They're still in their own country."

"Sure. Of course." Being interrupted seemed to annoy Derek Mercer. He'd been nearing a crescendo. "Point being, South Sudan, East Timor, all over Afghanistan, now here, I've learned one thing again and again, and it's what keeps me coming back to this racket: the power of the human spirit. It endures through all."

Pax didn't understand this man. How can you be a war reporter, he thought, and think that's the lesson?

"War breaks people," he said suddenly, which was followed by another intrusive thought: I know, because it broke me.

"Well, yes. Yet what was it Hemingway said?" Derek Mercer cleared his throat and, to Pax's ear, raised his voice several pitches. "Something like: 'Life breaks us all and afterward we can be stronger at the broken places.' That's been the homecoming journey for many veterans I know."

Pax knew he'd been challenged, or dismissed, or something, and he wanted to respond, even felt compelled to, but the sound of jazz music severed that pursuit. If I'm hearing jazz, he thought, that means no one else is speaking. Which means . . . he glanced out at the octagonal room and saw that everyone else, in all the other groups, was watching them, listening, Yeva and the aid workers and the old Boyko parents, too. "Sure, I guess so," he said, which seemed to placate most people, because they returned to their little circles of conversation. A man with narrow shoulders and a long, pallid face kept at it, though. It was the Judge, and he stayed looking at Pax well after everyone else had stopped.

Pax thought about excusing himself to the bathroom but didn't want it to seem like he needed to collect himself. So he stood there and held his cherry brandy, letting the others change the subject.

A crash ricocheted down the stairs, followed by the sight of a tumbling human bowling ball. A very pink-faced and disoriented Roman appeared, rising from the floor. He straightened his glasses, then spread out his arms like a degenerate Christ. "Heroyam slava!" he called.

The room applauded. Yeva shouted again at her brother. Derek Mercer checked the time on his wristwatch.

"When's the mayor due to arrive?" he asked Olek.

"His office canceled this morning. Yeva didn't tell you? Some virtual conference with Kyiv."

Derek Mercer didn't waste a moment. "Gentlemen," he said, "enjoy the evening." Then he was off, thanking Yeva and out the front door as Roman bowed to renewed applause.

Pax still felt like an errant stray but he'd come here to see Svitlana. He wasn't about to turn back now.

"I'm sorry about all that," he said to what remained of their circle.

Olek gripped his forearm. "I brought it up," he said. Not true but it's a nice thing to say, Pax thought. That was sometimes the thing about lies. They could be nice.

He asked Andrei about his organization. It was called Nove Zavtra, the man said, "New Tomorrow," founded during the crucible of Maidan. He was a field representative for it, a blanket term that involved delivering aid to the front, evacuating civilians to the Lviv train station, and organizing caches in the eastern villages so deliveries weren't a free-for-all. "I drove a refrigerated van with insulin to Dnipro yesterday," Andrei said. "Fifteen hours, no stop. Forty checkpoints."

"Courage Juice keep you awake?"

Andrei grinned. "Magnum Apple is the best flavor."

"What's it like? Out there, I mean."

The Ukrainian's grin fell away. "The road signs have been

spray-painted black or turned upside down to confuse the in-vaders. Every checkpoint looks for saboteurs. Night is darker than dark. Days, you can see, but that is also a curse. Their tanks shoot at cars with families, kids and pets in the back. They run over people on bicycles for sport. I have observed this. It is . . ."

He stopped there.

Even talk of the zero line made Pax's skin raise, made him worry for Lee. There was artillery, and missiles, the enemy controlled the sky, it was so different than even the worst days they'd fought through in Wardak. Under this worry was something else, though. It crackled and bayed and ultimately soothed. Under his worry for his friend lay relief for himself.

Andrei regained a verbal stride. "There is this tension, it is impossible to explain. I was there, yesterday. Now I am here, in this beautiful home, drinking and appreciating."

Pax asked why he'd gone into humanitarian work.

The response came slowly. "I needed to see that others were worse off than me," he said.

Maybe this is it, Pax thought. Maybe this is how I can help. I might be broken but I'm not useless. He asked who he could speak with about volunteering.

Andrei blinked at him, his English bent in uncertainty. "Yeva! She is the founder of Nove Zavtra. You know this, yes?

It is why we're here. It is how we know her, how we know Svitlana and Taras."

Pax sputtered out an attempt at comprehension, thinking and realizing that Taras must be Chernenko and Chernenko, Taras. Andrei pulled a smartphone from his pocket. "Taras just sent us this. To raise funds from the West."

And there he was, Chernenko in the digital flesh, Mr. Svitlana, Pax's life enemy he'd barely known even existed, standing in front of the ruins of a brick house. "Thank you for delivering us first-aid kits to our people," he said, quivers of wind audible through the video. "We are located in Kherson region, near the zero line. Ukraine is in very hard situation, and having such friends as you, who are caring about our lives, is very important, thank you, guys." He was bald, of medium stature, with a simple gray beard. He wore cammies and black, ballistic sunglasses and held an AK with blue and yellow tape wrapped around its stock. "We are fighting for freedom, not only for Ukraine, but for all civilized"—the audio cut out, then returned—"we fight monsters. Thank you for who you are." He didn't look like a lawyer. And he didn't sound like an enemy, not Pax's, anyhow. He looked like a guy who'd seen and done some shit and now wanted to come home, or at least sleep a few hours. Pax looked for a ring on the man's hand. It was too grainy to make out what he considered the state of his marriage. "In the future, tomorrow, or the next day or next, we will push them back to the hell which they did come." More wind shuddered, overwhelming whatever was said next. He raised his AK to the camera and flashed a peace sign. The video screen faded to black.

I don't belong here. That was Pax's first thought. Then he saw Svitlana emerge from the staircase. She wore a long black chemise he didn't recognize and conch shell earrings he did and he could tell by the wetness in her eyes and reapplied mascara that she'd been crying.

Yet I'll stay, was his second thought. Andrei was waiting for a reaction to the video, so he said, "Cool." Then he went to her.

"You okay?" he asked.

"Hi," Svitlana said. "I'm sorry to have left you alone. You've managed?"

He'd stepped too close. She slid a pace back. He did the same.

"Luke Paxton. How have you been? It's been years."

"Ten." Why not, he thought. "Since my midtour leave. Since Milan."

"Let's catch up," she said, ignoring the reference. There was cheer in her voice, Pax thought. It sounded forced, sure, but it was there. "I want to hear all about your life."

He didn't want to tell her how everything had gone wrong since Milan, but he didn't know how not to. Returning to Afghanistan had been the hardest part but it wasn't like he'd ever not have. What'd come after, though, those had been choices. Trying school, failing out. Trying jobs, quitting them. Trying the VA, quitting it. Trying school again, failing out again. Boozing too much, fighting too often, saying he'd turned a corner, believing he'd turned a corner, then waking up in the same pits, with the same pities. Packing up and going to a new place, in a new state, to do it all again the same way.

"Ladies first," he said, smiling wide, watching the conch shells dangle from her ears. Cinque Terre, he thought. She got those there.

"Well," she began, and then Yeva was shouting in Ukrainian, and the various clusters of guests started shuffling to an adjacent room.

"Later," Svitlana said, touching the top of Pax's hand with her fingers. Tremors like light raced up his arm. "Yeva gets outrageous when people don't listen to her." Then she was gone, and the hostess was in his ear saying that she'd seated him on the far side of the dinner table, next to the Judge. "He's eager to visit with you," and Pax was fine with that, he could talk with old people, until he saw that Svitlana was on the other end of the table, seats away, which might as well have been an ocean away, and it again felt like the world was in great conspiracy against him.

He brushed past the aid workers, who were still exuding disdain. At least they didn't put me with them, he thought. The Judge stood behind his chair, waiting. They shook hands and the older man's grip proved firm. They took their seats.

"English?" Pax asked.

The Judge winced. He held up a phone the size of a gaming console and then typed into it. "Tonight I am this old man's tongue," a sultry, robotic voice said. Pax gave a thumbs-up.

Across from them sat Unknown, also exiled to the far end of the table, his ponderous gaze fixed up, toward the room's chandeliers. Wrought-iron lions gleamed there against the dull light. The three Boyko siblings gathered around their parents at the center of the table, calling for everyone's attention. Pax looked catty-corner from him, where Svitlana sat. She was straight-backed, on the lip of her chair. She was chewing the tips of her straw hair, a habit that meant she was lost in thought, which he'd forgotten about but now remembered.

Not Cinque Terre, Pax thought. She got those shell earrings in Capri. Which is where we—

Yeva began in a roar of thick Ukrainian. Andrei called out, "English!" and as the whole table shifted Pax's way, he added, "Not for him, for me!" which earned some laughter.

They settled on Yeva speaking, Olek translating, and Roman standing between them, a half step behind, blinking away under his glasses.

"We still wait for one more but must start before the food cools! Thank you for joining us, old friends and new. Any act of normalcy during this madness is an act of courage. For that, we thank you.

"There is nothing special about today, except that all days are special, when we can be free to speak ideas, safe to—"

"Yes there is," Roman interrupted his sister. Yeva sighed, then turned to him and yielded the room.

"It's International Women's Day."

"What?"

"It's International Women's Day." Roman smiled, more to himself than anything, and raised his glass of vodka. "To the females!" he said.

Everyone laughed, no one harder or longer than his mother. They all toasted to the females.

"In Ukraine, we have glory to the idea of the defender," Olek said. "It is linked to who we are." He raised his glass. "To the defenders! Do Zakhysnyka!"

They toasted to the defenders.

"Until victory!" Yeva's toast. And they toasted to victory.

Roman took his seat while his siblings began carrying

in appetizer plates. He looked across at Pax. "Hope you like squirrel brain," he said. "Ukrainian gourmet."

The Judge shook his head and typed into his phone. "His parents had him too late," it said. "They were too tired for discipline. It is why he is like this."

The appetizers arrived, marinated cucumbers and cabbage rolls and a boiled dumpling Pax called a pierogi but was told wasn't. He drank some water to sober up some, then switched to the vodka, a triple-filtered, corn-based spirit from Odesa strong enough to pop his ears.

"Where in America do you hail?" the Judge asked through his phone. He seemed to understand English well enough even as he wasn't comfortable speaking it.

"Tulsa," Pax said. "Oil country."

"Ahh, Texas. I have always wished to visit."

Pax went along with it. It seemed close enough.

"I believe we've walked the same mountains," the Judge continued, pausing to sip from his own glass of vodka. "You soldiered in Afghanistan?"

Pax tilted his head. "Yeah," he said. "Wardak Province, 2011 and '12." Oh shit, he realized. The Red Army. "Where were you?"

"Kunduz. 1987. Before you were a dream in your parents' eyes."

He'd trained on tanks but ended up in a motorized rifle regiment, arriving in-country as a replacement during the throes of fighting season. "Your government had begun sending Stinger missiles during this time. Many Soviet pilots were being shot down."

The Judge's initial brush with combat had come his very first week: "It was a long patrol, escorting fuel trucks. We entered a narrow valley and immediately came under heavy fire. Those were our guns, of course, captured, now being used against us."

"What else has stayed with you?"

"Once we caught shepherds smuggling machine guns under their sheep's bellies." Pax laughed at that memory. "Another time, we entered a dugout captured from the bandits. I went to take a thermos flask from the corner. As a trophy, it was a nice flask. My commander saved me, unscrewed its bottom, and black goo fell out. Material that only needed my hot tea poured in to become an explosive."

Pax smiled at that anecdote once the Judge did first.

"But I was one of the lucky ones. The war mostly happened to me. Choices, right or wrong, were for others. I knew I could come back to regular life, go to university, I just needed to survive. The worst thing that happened, I only saw." The Judge stopped to consider his words for translation. "A woman standing outside our base, holding an infant in her arms. The baby had died two days before. Not from the war, not a battle, at least. Sickness in her lungs. But the mother refused to let go. The little body had gone rigid and turned blue." The Judge waited for the phone to finish its work, his long face solemn under the chandelier light.

"Jesus."

"When we returned home, there was a small gathering of families who had lost their sons and husbands. Not a protest, not what an American would call one. But they wanted to be there and wanted us to know they were there, so maybe they would get more truth about what had happened to their soldier. And as clear as you are to me now: I saw that Afghan mother in that group of Ukrainian and Russian women, staring into our shame."

"No way." Pax chewed over what he'd been told. It was too incredible to not believe. "Ever see her again?"

"Once." The Judge sat back and crossed one leg over another, folding his arms across his chest. "Some years later, I was a young attorney, visiting the grave of a childhood friend. He hadn't died in the war but was one of those who never got over it. I looked down the line of headstones, thinking about why some of us could move on and others did not, and there she was again, cradling a baby in her arms, or something like it." The Judge waited again for the phone. "Then she gestured at me to join them."

Pax realized he'd been holding his breath. "What did she want?"

"I'll never know." The Judge's posture held firm but his voice betrayed him, Pax heard it wobble even through the language divide. "It was the first choice I made in the war, and I fled from it as fast as I could.

"She will be there when death comes for me, this I know in my heart."

Pax clung to the quiet, thinking. He'd known ghosts existed in Afghanistan, he'd felt them, too. But to be followed home by one . . . he clinked the Judge's glass with his own and then asked why he'd shared with him tonight.

The phone's robotic voice returned: "People will spend the rest of your life trying to tell you how to feel about your war." The Judge's long face held firm under the chandelier light. "Do not let them."

Pax tried to find something to say, then found Lee's words spilling out of his mouth. "Gotta let it go. Otherwise it'll eat you up from inside, and the enemy gets another tally."

The Judge nodded but the smile it came with never seemed to reach his eyes.

It was disturbing, being with this old man still haunted by

his war. He's a judge, Pax thought, who's led a successful life, but he doesn't want to talk about that, or his family, or his home that's under siege. Pax saw a glimpse of himself doing the same thing, decades from now, telling the same story about Private First Class Shiloh and Captain Merriman and the checkpoint. He looked over at Svitlana. She was talking away with Andrei and was beautiful and lovely and he was seeing her again. She was not the girl he'd once known but a formed person with a formed life. She had a flower bed, and a son. She was a person with a past and he was part of the past, it was why he was here tonight. But so what? I need to prove, he thought, that I can and will move on. And then maybe I can.

The Judge was talking about bringing Pax to Kyiv, when it was safe again. He wanted to make him an honorary member of their Afghan Veterans Association chapter. Pax said he'd like that, because he now felt bad for the old man, because he could never change, but I still can, Pax thought, and something loosened deep inside him.

"Just get to tomorrow," he said. It had nothing to do with what the Judge was going on about but Pax was compelled to share. "Used to tell myself that on rough days in Wardak. Probably need to start doing it again."

The Judge's eyes splintered. Then he pointed across the table. "Tomorrow in Ukraine, boys like this may have to fight like the Afghan bandits." He laughed at his own observation and Pax smiled along. Roman answered them with a tiny glare.

Svitlana announced something to the table in Ukrainian, then moved into the other room. Music emerged seconds later; an instrumental jam-band song Pax knew from Vicenza barracks parties. He'd kept her away from those—you never took women you cared about to the barracks—yet here it was, a decade later, being played in a manor on the outskirts of Lviv. It'd been stripped of its lyrics so he hummed along to the tune. She returned to the dining room and smiled across at him. He held the olives of her eyes with his own.

"These are morose times," she said. "But we do not need to be morose."

"Our Svita," Yeva said with mock disapproval. "Our culture has never been good enough for her!"

Svitlana denied that but the table had been lost. "Now I know why the neighborhood children shout in American curse words," Olek said. "Their language tutor teaches them from rock music!"

Most of the table laughed. "Oh, fuck off!" Svitlana said, which caused even more laughter.

Yeva asked Svitlana to help her bring in the main dishes. The front door yawned open, an echoing, masculine voice rushing the warmth of the house. Pax heard people say a name and rise from the table to greet the arrival but he couldn't make sense of it, none of it aligned, and he was still disbelieving and confused as a man with a sandy beard stepped through the dining room, shaking people's hands, giving them hugs, kissing Olek the architect on the lips, a quick kiss but real one, a full one, and then Pax found himself being noticed in the corner, and assessed.

"Corporal Paxton. Hello." It was Bogdan, the recruiter, his English ever-jagged yet ever-clear. "It is strange to find you here. But good."

A faint ripple of hesitation was moving through the Ukrainian man's icy stare. It was hard to see, Pax thought, but there.

"Nice to see you, as well," he said. "My friend is getting along?"

"Yes," Bogdan said, opening out to the table. "Corporal Paxton was of great help yesterday with a new legion fighter." He turned back to Pax. "Your friend is safe, with the right people."

Pax nodded. At the table, only Roman seemed to be listening for more. Bogdan did not allow this void to deepen.

"I heard a joke today," he said. "A Russian rifleman, tanker, and pilot are returning to Moscow from the front. Who is driving?"

He paused a beat, looking around at the others. "The coroner."

The table didn't laugh so much as it cheered. Svitlana returned to the room holding plates. When she delivered Pax his, he tugged at the lobe of his own ear and stared at her, hard, until she looked back.

"Capri," he said. "Right?"

She remembered. He could tell by the way her eyes turned in and her lips curled up that she did. It had been a good trip. Not that they'd seen much of the island. It had rained most of their time there. And their villa had been stocked with a delicious wine that tasted like citrus. It'd paired well with oysters. And bare skin.

"I don't recall," she said.

"I do," Pax said. He'd maxed out two credit cards for Capri but it had been worth it. The 173rd deployed to Afghanistan the month after. Memories of that trip and others had sustained him until midtour leave. Until Milan.

"Enjoy your dinner," she said.

It was breaded chicken stuffed with cheese and vegetables and there was potato salad and garlic rolls. Pax ate with abandon because he was hungry and because he knew it was the only way to keep drunkenness at bay. The adherence to English at the table slipped, but Pax didn't mind, he was mostly elsewhere during the meal, on an island in the Mediterranean a decade before. That was it, he thought. If Milan was where it all went wrong Capri was where all of it was right. She's wearing those earrings tonight on purpose.

Pax's vision drifted across the table, where he caught the woman from the UN observing him. He tried a grin, mid-bite. She only blinked in response and returned to her own plate.

What the hell? Pax thought. What did I do to these people?

Conversation at the table had turned heavy. Pax tried to home in on its specifics, which drew the attention of one of its principals. Olek motioned toward him, the folds in the man's forehead bending with deliberation.

"You might have a good answer to this: What does a man do after war? How can we better prepare our veterans for life after?"

"Wow, well. Big question." Pax dared not look at Svitlana while he answered, nor at any of the aid workers. He didn't know what to say, other than not saying, "War breaks people." Nope, don't say that, he thought, no one here wants to hear that. Pull it together, he told himself. Pull it together and don't fuck up.

Then he thought of something.

"Speaking only for myself, the army is where I learned to

work on engines." It was so simple, he thought, because it was true. "It took me a while to figure it out, but war gave me a vocation. I'm a car mechanic back home, and well . . ." The cherry brandy sang in his blood and now he looked directly at the aid workers. "I'm good at it because I learned to fix Humvees in a very stressful environment."

At his side, the Judge nodded, and farther down the table, Pax heard someone vocalize agreement. To his surprise, it was Bogdan.

"A mechanic," Bogdan said. "A useful skill."

"Vocations, yes, that's the word," Olek added. "The mayor will like that."

"Perhaps this makes me a bad citizen," Roman cut in, slouched back in his chair, his voice acerbic, "but shouldn't our government leaders focus on achieving the victory instead of whatever comes after?"

Only now did Pax sense an invisible friction present at the table.

Bogdan said something in Ukrainian, something under his breath but also not. Roman shifted toward it like an animal to a whistle. He peered at the older man from under his glasses.

"Does the Commander have something to say to me?"

Bogdan sneered back. "Since you ask: the president has

called for a million-man army. He should have three million by now. This fight belongs to us all. It will find us all."

Olek put a hand on Bogdan's forearm while raising his other toward his brother, palm out. It did not work.

"Ahh, another talk about who is worthy and who is not." Roman leaned up from his slouch. "The Donbas might as well be another planet to me. But I do read. I know the unity you speak of comes with dirt and grime we're not supposed to discuss in front of our international friends. Ultras and supremacists fight for Ukraine, too, and for all your chatter, they'd hang you right alongside the invaders. A homosexual patriot is still a homosexual, dear Commander.

"Yes, yes, you lost your legs out there. And for that we all must listen to you drone on every dinner. You made your sacrifice. Now we make ours.

"You infer me a pacificist. I am no such thing. No Ukrainian could be now. I simply know the truth: I am no soldier. I would be useless in such a place, a burden to those who can fight. But where should I go? I must stay here, by order of law and shame. And I will. I walk away from the Moldovan gangs who offer journeys out, even though my mother here would gladly pay their price. Is this not enough for you? I stay so you can jeer and look down on me, the man who cannot fight, even for his family's survival.

"I want others to fight for me, to save my life, to keep my life the way it is." He nodded at Pax. "He said dumb wars get dumb endings. Correct, because all wars do." He wasn't even in the room when I said that, Pax thought. Word had obviously gotten around. "Leave it alone, Commander. Already the reservists mobilize. In a few months, they'll get to us, the cripples and the cowards, and we'll march east, together. Until that day comes, leave me alone."

Roman's glasses had slid down the bridge of his nose during his speech. He pushed them back into position, then looked up and away from the table, into the wrought-iron lions of the chandeliers. Pax exhaled through his nostrils and glanced over to Bogdan. A wicked leer had taken hold of the man.

"See, there is fight in you," Bogdan said. Then he stood up and began clearing the table.

Someone needed to say something, everyone knew it, everyone felt it. Pax heard muffled Ukrainian coming from the far side of the Judge; it was the white-haired matriarch of the Boyko clan, who'd spent much of the meal watching and listening. Yeva and then Svitlana were talking back to her, shaking their heads. Faces kept turning Pax's way.

"What is it?"

Svitlana shook her head again but Yeva relented. "You do not have to answer her."

"It's all good. Whatever."

"She wishes to know about this." She pointed at her wrist, causing Pax to look down at his own. Then she pantomimed his frantic tic.

Not this shit, Pax thought, seeing Bogdan come into the room and depart with more plates, not again. He moved both hands under his thighs and searched for an excuse. He held the room's attention now, as a way to forget about the argument between their gay, militant in-law and their lazy, wayward son. Pax felt the crush of judgment all over again, except now Svitlana was here, watching him with utter interest, some residue skepticism, too, her eyes quivering, and he knew instinctually what he needed to do, it was obvious as smoke. He would not let himself stand in the way of what he sought, not again. He took a slow yoga breath and smiled his most American smile, all big teeth and dopey energy, and sat up straight against his chair.

"In Afghanistan," he began, "I made friends with a young boy named Ali. He gifted me these before we left, and they've become very special to me."

Pax knew when to pause, to reflect, when to laugh about the capitalist spirit in the child and how to leave dangling his dark, unknown fate. He didn't need to add, "Like here." It was already in the room, pervasive and full and smothering. Yeva translated. At no point did he explain why he thumbed

the beads as he did, nor did he try to. That lay in the con-
text. It was the kind of war story people wanted. Tenderness
in devastation. It was the kind of war story people expected.
Fellowship amidst ruin.

Some of the Ukrainians clapped when he was done, for
him, for Ali, too. Svitlana was chewing the tips of her hair
and the Judge put a hand on his shoulder. Even the aid workers looked impressed.

"You are a good man, Mister Graves," Yeva said, and Pax
couldn't remember the last time someone had said that to him.

———

Later, after the Judge had gone home and the senior Boykos
had retired to bed and Roman had gone upstairs to play
video games and everyone remaining had gathered in the
octagonal room for coffees or nightcaps, Svitlana sat next to
Pax on the couch.

"You were great tonight," she said. "Thank you. I hope you
enjoyed yourself?"

He thought about that. The awkwardness of his arrival,
and most everything that had happened since, felt weeks
gone, not hours. Across the room, Bogdan raised his drink
to him. They had a tacit understanding now, Pax thought,
keepers of one another's secrets.

"Yes," he told Svitlana. "Weird night. But glad I came."

"The argument was very much," she said. "You got the full Ukrainian experience."

"I don't know. The freedom to do nothing. Isn't that the dream?"

Svitlana dismissed that with a wave of her hand. "Do not think Roman is indicative of anything but himself. Ukrainians are patriots. And real ones, not the loud American type. We will turn Lviv into a resistance city for a hundred years if we must."

"I believe it." Pax settled into his confidence. "Let's drop the war." He paused. "How do you know these crazy people?"

She laughed. "Yeva and I became friends as Young Pioneers. I should apologize about her. She is the best in so many ways. What she's done with Nove Zavtra is amazing. I love her."

"She keeps calling me Mister Graves?"

Svitlana popped her tongue off the roof of her mouth. "A joke about foreign soldiers," she said. "Harmless," she added.

Pax left that alone. "I heard a 'but' coming."

Svitlana looked around the room to make sure no one was eavesdropping. "She likes me and she likes my husband and she wants our marriage to survive more than either of us does."

Pax almost reached for her hand in that moment but

knew she was shy in public with these things. Had been, at least, getting her alone had always been the game, the pursuit. Still, this was the first time she'd directly mentioned her marriage. It seemed a step forward, and Pax knew he had Ali to thank for it. He leaned forward, nudging himself inches closer, again smelling traces of her coconut shampoo. The song from the loudspeaker ended. A familiar acoustic scratching replaced it.

"Hey," he said, pointing up to the air. "It's your song."

"What?" she said.

"'In the Aeroplane Over the Sea.'"

She tilted her head to listen. "I remember," she said. Then her eyes narrowed. "It was your favorite."

Pax leaned back. "No! It was yours. It's fine. A little whiny for me, if I'm being honest."

That made Svitlana smirk. Not smile, Pax thought, but smirk. "Luke Paxton, you loved whiny music!"

"You think you know someone." He rubbed at his head. "Then this comes out."

Svitlana tightened her mouth a bit, not, Pax noticed, without a little circumspection. "If I hadn't been home," she began, before starting again, "If we'd departed Ukraine. What would you have done?"

"Oh." Pax scrunched his face, thinking, and to show that

he was thinking. The figment of Barcelona seemed more nebulous than ever. "I'm sure I'd have found something."

Svitlana was the last to leave, well past midnight. Yeva had needed not so much to talk with her but at her, an unfiltered rant about different volunteer militias that had been approaching Nove Zavtra to help run supplies to the front. Weapons? No, of course not. Unless you're okay with that. Unless you consider drones and body armor and radios, weapons. And since we're here, Yeva Boyko, how do you feel about microchips and memory cards tucked away in tampons and medical bandages? And bullets?

Some of the groups were fine. Others not. Of course those had been the ones offering the most financial compensation. No small matter for a grassroots nonprofit with limited reach to the West. Svitlana was Yeva's pragmatic friend. She'd played her role as she knew she'd needed to, even while knowing Yeva would never relent. Her old friend, God bless her, still believed in right and wrong.

Svitlana had half expected Luke Paxton to be waiting at her car. He wasn't. Am I relieved? she thought. Yes. Maybe. She wasn't sure. There was a reckless hunger in his face she didn't trust. The boy she remembered seemed mostly gone, a bashful, reluctant soldier who'd won her over with a persistence and sincerity she'd never known what to do with. He'd listened to her more than any man she'd ever met, really listened, held actual interest in her thoughts and ideas. And he'd always been able to make her laugh. That person had reappeared tonight, in glimmers, usually when he was talking to someone other than her. Endearing, in a way. Obnoxious in another.

We were lovers once, she thought, turning on her car. So what. Men pretended sex was just sex until they decided it was everything else, as well.

Yeva had called him a good man. Svitlana considered that. She didn't find it such a trivial thing anymore. She also knew it wasn't the only thing.

The story of the Afghan boy and the beads had been compelling. She'd never heard it before. But something had happened during her call with Taras, a couple people had mentioned it, Luke Paxton had apparently shouted down the reporter. My fault, she thought. Walking into that room by himself couldn't have been easy.

Then there'd been that odd moment with the earrings. Capri? Taras had bought them for her in Odesa three Christmases prior. And why was Luke even here? He kept deflecting the basic question. He still carried himself with the latent violence she remembered from Milan. Going there then had been a mistake but he'd guilted her into it. His mentions of it tonight . . . why? What drove men to wallow in the past the way they did? Taras did similar. It wasn't serious, Svitlana thought. The past was all sentiment and revision.

Luke Paxton had never raised his hand to her, though. There was that.

Svitlana looked at the clock on the dashboard. How? she thought. When did it get this late? The sitter would be streaming Eurovision on the couch and filled with righteous, youthful fury, she wasn't sure she had enough money in her pocketbook to quell it. Denys better have stayed asleep, she thought, all the while knowing he hadn't. Ever since Taras had gone east, the boy always ended up in her bed, cuddling up his bony body against the nightmares.

V

Tuesday had been the night of the dinner party. On Wednesday, Pax found the grocery store and exchanged some dollars for hryvnia at the bank. On Thursday, he figured out the flat's washing machine and called Yeva, then texted with Lee over an encrypted messaging app the other man insisted they use. On Friday, he woke at daybreak to the sound of a phone alert. It was from Svitlana.

"Great seeing you the other night! I don't know if you are still in Lviv let alone free/awake but my car won't start . . ."

He told her he'd be there in fifteen minutes.

He arrived in forty, twisted around by a morning express tram. He jogged from the cemetery and found her sitting in the driver's seat of a posh hatchback, bundled up in her hooded jacket like a defeated pilgrim.

"Sorry," he said, trying not to breathe too loud. He'd known he was no longer in fighting shape and now felt it in his legs and chest. "Still figuring out the rhythms here."

"Did you do this?" She pointed to the front of her car. He'd read her text as suppliant, even coy, but her voice carried daggers in it.

"What?"

"Did you break my car so I'd need your help?"

"Come on," he said. "Your friend has street cameras. I saw them, rich people are the same everywhere. Second, how would I get access? You lock your car? Third, you drove home that night. I'd have disconnected a battery cable, no car can move a foot then. Or a meter. Whatever."

He left out how he'd learned that particular trick. It was a simple way to keep someone from driving home drunk, and had been done to him. Svitlana crossed her arms and mumbled something low he couldn't make out. She doesn't believe me, he thought. Unbelievable.

"Pop the hood." God help me, Pax thought, if it actually is a disconnected cable. "Shouldn't take long to diagnose."

Both the battery and alternator belt seemed fine. The car was overdue for an oil change but that had nothing to do with it. He almost asked if she'd run out of gas but she didn't appear in a kidding mood. All the wires and hoses held; the spark plugs were in place, as was the ECU fuse, once he found it, at least, he wasn't too familiar with Czech engines. He wondered if she'd done this to get him to come out this morning. That seemed far-fetched given the strain on her face, even as he liked the idea. He asked if she'd tried a spare key. She went inside for one and returned to the driver's seat. The engine grumbled awake.

"That can happen," he said. "The transponder in some of these new keys goes bad, then the car won't recognize them."

"It was the key."

"It was the key."

"My hero," she said sarcastically, a blend of embarrassment and relief. He shut the hood and walked to the car door. She looked up. "I am grateful. But of course this happens on a busy morning, and of course it was the stupid key."

"Now I get to call you 'Gypsy' again. That's the price."

"Hah."

"Hah." He was going to ask what she had going on today when the sound of a metal gate popped open from behind them. He turned to find a boy about seven or eight approaching. The child was built like a reed and looking at him with chary interest. Straw, black hair shaped into bangs and a sharp jawline left no doubt who his mother was.

"Khto ty?" The boy's voice cracked.

"English," Svitlana said from the car.

"Who are you?"

"My name's Luke." Pax held out his hand. The boy shook it with all the formality he could muster. "Old friend of your mom's."

"From where? She's never been to America." The boy's face scrunched. "Has she?"

"Italy. Long time ago." Which was true, Pax thought, and also not. It all depended.

The boy watched Pax from the sides of his eyes rather than straight on; he possessed a guardedness that belied the clean shine of his face.

"What's your name?"

"Denys."

"What grade you in, Denys?" Talking to kids was like talking to old people, Pax thought. Pepper them with questions.

"Grade Two." A pride entered the boy's words. "I go to the international school."

"How's that going?" Pax didn't mean anything with his question. He only wanted to know.

"Class is virtual now." Svitlana stepped out of the car and

around Pax, touching the small of his back as she did so. "Just like the pandemic, and Mrs. Solomko has done a nice job of maintaining routine. Did you finish your worksheets?"

The boy nodded.

"All of them?"

The boy nodded again.

"Have you fed Elvis?"

Denys's mouth puckered and his eyes fell to his feet.

Svitlana said something firm and demanding in Ukrainian. Denys turned with a subtle reluctance. When he reached the gate he looked back at Pax.

"Elvis is our cat," he explained.

"I figured," Pax said.

"We are going to the chocolate house this evening," the boy said. "I hope you can come. It is my favorite place in the world."

Pax looked at Svitlana, who remained stone-faced. "Thanks. Nice meeting you."

"Seems like a good kid," he said, once Denys had returned inside. "His English is great."

"He is hungry for male attention." Svitlana paused. "He misses his father very much."

"Of course. He's at that age." Pax watched as she reached for a strand of hair to chew, then caught herself. "I'm working for Yeva today at the train station. Volunteering."

"I heard." Pax waited for an expression of gratitude that never came. She was squinting at him as if trying to see him through a shadow, the hood of her jacket framing her scrutiny.

Had she been like this when they were young? Maybe not so much but yeah, he allowed, she'd always been careful. We all became what we used to be but more, he thought. What once were quirks are now traits, our full selves have emerged through it all. I'm sure I'm no different.

"Join us tonight. It's in the district the young people like. It'll be good for Denys and my way of saying thank you for the car."

"Do you want me to come? That's the question."

The olives in her eyes flashed, and her posture relaxed with it. "Yes," she said. This time, it was Pax who couldn't hold the gaze.

_____

As Pax waited for a tram, another air-raid siren blared. They'd been happening four, five, eight times a day, and no one around him paid it any bother. Still, the auditory shrill of it did something to his brain, fizzing, sensory overload well beyond the scope of duloxetine. He needed something to focus on. He pulled out his phone and reread his text exchange with Lee.

His friend had made it to Yavoriv, where an old NATO training center in the middle of a forest was collecting legionnaires. Lee hadn't wanted to discuss it much, even through the encrypted app—Pax had asked how the training was, and instead received a flurry of messages thanking him for coming over.

"You're the only one who got it." And, "Everyone else had fucking excuses." And, "Some shitbirds be mad at us for coming, you know that? Cuz it makes them look at their reasons for staying and see them for what they are. Weak-ass bullshit."

They'd wanted him to fail, Lee continued, wanted him to be a clown, a stupid, lost goon, because that would validate their own inaction. Fuck them, he said, and their lack of fucking stones. We're the doers. We're the men in the arena.

The diatribe had read nervous to Pax, which made sense. There'd been a media report about new, disorganized foreign units around Kyiv getting shelled by Russian artillery and overrun by tanks. So he'd replied with Lee's own quote back at him: "'For what are we born if not to aid one another?' Some don't wait to be told. Some just go," which earned a "Roger that" and thumbs-up emoji from Lee. Pax had wanted to tell him about Nove Zavtra but had held back. There was nothing to share. He hadn't done a damn thing yet.

He got off the tram and looked around to orient himself.

Mackerel clouds gave the day some thin cover while a chapping wind smacked of Eastern European severity. Pax took a slow yoga breath and tucked his chin into his coat. If nothing else, he'd learned to layer here. Through the wind and the air came steady waves of mass chatter. He walked to the sound of the sound.

Pax turned a corner and the train station was posted sentinel across the cityscape, horizontal and wide. Its cool gray dome loomed over pavilions of alabaster yellow. The front square of the station teemed with medical tents and food stalls and big, laminated signs for buses to Poland and Germany. As Pax neared it he thought there must be hundreds of people milling about, then corrected that to thousands. As he entered the crush, he passed a man in a Red Cross vest and hat holding out a bin of stuffed animals for a little girl to choose from, and then saw the line of dozens of families waiting for the same. Across the path was another line for diapers. Maybe tens of thousands, he thought, if you include what's in the station. It was almost all women and kids, minus various volunteers and guardsmen. He saw little dogs in carriers and hamsters in pockets and birds in cages and cats on leashes. Pax couldn't move fast nor could he move slow, the crowd guided and maintained its rhythm, its own pace. But there was order amidst the chaos. He found the predictability in it soothing. There was nothing to do now but be another person.

He was supposed to meet Andrei at the fountain but couldn't spot him. He leaned against a lamppost to wait. Dozens of haggard-looking people with cords and phones clumped around a nearby mobile cart of electrical sockets. There was a sandwich station and a yogurt station and another for juice boxes and bottled water. To his front, about seventy feet and under the shade of the pavilion, an old woman played the piano. It sounded classical, Pax thought, Beethoven or Chopin or something. He listened some more. Nope, he realized. That's "Let It Be."

In assembly there was resolve, in singular elements, sorrow. Over there was a young mother breastfeeding under a shawl, grim-faced as a skull. Over there, a volunteer in a bright yellow vest smoking a nub down to its cherry. Over there were bodies in sleeping bags, the remnants of their lives in surrounding boxes and suitcases. Between them a figure mopped at a smear of cement, wet outlines forming in the wake.

The highs and lows were too much. Pax had no choice but to observe in a diminished mode. Focus on something, he thought, so he watched a bird, another one of the loud, midnight-blue magpies, circle low around the food stalls. It saw nothing worth pursuing and cawed through the wind.

That's a Lee bird, Pax thought. It's saying, Fuck you, jabro-nis, I'm here, know that.

The smell of human stink blitzed Pax from the side and then a man in a soccer jersey was grabbing at him. He had wavy hair the color of soot and heavy bags under his eyes and was demanding something in hoarse words that weren't English but weren't Ukrainian, either. Pax stepped back and pushed off the man's fingers but then the man grabbed him with his other hand at the top of his coat, and his demands kept on coming in a language that pattered like a stream. Pax didn't know what else to do so he pulled out his wallet and tossed down a couple bills and repeated, "I'm here to help, I'm here to help."

Then Andrei was there, barking in a tone Pax hadn't thought the volunteer capable of. He stepped between Pax and the other man. The pattering continued. So did Andrei.

"What's he want?"

"Crazy person, I am sorry, Mister Paxton!"

"Not at all." Pax put his hand on Andrei's forearm to try to calm him. "I think he needs help, is all."

Andrei's nostrils flared but asked the other man to explain himself. More pattering ensued.

"Like I say, a crazy person. He wishes to use a phone to locate his sister, but all the connections are down in the east.

I try to tell him another phone will not work but he does not listen. The vatnik horde destroys the mobile towers."

They tried anyhow. The call would not go through. The man in the soccer jersey said something hostile. Andrei responded full-throated and red-faced.

The man spat on the ground where Pax's money lay. Then he beelined for the train station itself, as if shot from a cannon. Pax waited a few seconds, then asked, "What was that about?"

"He called me a tin-potted Carpathian . . . slur from Maidan, it does not matter. He is uncivilized person from the mines region."

"How could you even understand him? That wasn't Ukrainian. Was it?"

Andrei smiled with his teeth. "That slushing was Surzhyk. A mix of language. Part Russian, part Ukrainian, all uncivilized." Then he looked down at the spit near his feet and cursed at himself.

"Ahh, fucks to the hell. He is my countryman. I am a Carpathian punk, he is right. I was mad for not being on time to gather you. Please stay here, I will return."

He strode out after the man in the soccer jersey. If there'd been remedy made, or not, he made no mention of it when he came back minutes later. In the meantime, Pax had collected the money from the ground. It seemed a waste to just let it sit there.

Andrei led Pax to a warehouse two blocks from the station. Industrial fans roared through the space, dozens of people trudging about in workwear. Pax recognized Unknown unloading wooden pallets from a forklift and gave a tiny wave. In response, the other man yielded the slightest hint of a nod.

Yeva approached them, wearing jeans and a crew-neck sweatshirt. Pax said hello but she disregarded the pleasantries.

"Can you read English?" she asked.

"My teachers didn't think so," Pax said. He thought she'd been joking. She was not. He corrected himself. "Yes, I'm fluent. No problem."

Yeva took him to a sequestered area in the rear of the warehouse where many boxes of mail shipments lay about. She pointed to a row of plastic bins nestled against the wall.

"Supplies for the golden hour. Tourniquets go there. Emergency airways there, clotting bandages in that one. Put any trauma shears on the table, any extra gauze here . . . do not mix occlusive dressing with pressure dressing. Needles for decomp there. Anything weird or unnecessary, put it in that bin. Once we get everything unpacked and separated, we will start compiling kits, but that is for tomorrow."

"Check, rog," he said. "Quick question."

"Quick," Yeva said. She seemed distracted.

"Your friends at the dinner. The aid workers." He'd been thinking about this much of the week. "They fucking hated me."

Yeva grimaced. "Not my friends. Potential partners, maybe. They . . ." She waved it away. "They thought you were someone else. Their mistake."

She didn't want to say who. It took some cajoling and eventually she relented.

"One of them had watched a video of an American soldier throwing a dog off a cliff. A puppy. For sport."

It took Pax a few seconds to understand what was being conveyed. "They thought that was me?"

"Yes." Yeva looked at him with a combination of pity and detachment. "I know it was not, we checked later. They felt very bad for being rude to you."

"That was a marine. I was army." Pax knew the video. They'd talked about it in basic as an example of what not to be like. "And it happened in Iraq. I served in Afghanistan."

Yeva shrugged. "Those differences matter to those who know them. Again, my apologies for their behavior. Sometimes you just cannot know why people believe what they do." She pressed a box cutter into his hand. "Be fast but exact," she said. Then she left.

The warehouse lay across gun-metal-gray concrete that

absorbed window light. The whirring of the large fans gave the space a constant melody. I've never been accused of puppy slaughter before, Pax thought, flicking open the box cutter. Not a great feeling.

He soon lost himself to the work. Most of the shipments were addressed from Western nations, many from hospitals and medical organizations, but some seemed like personal donations, combat tourniquets pulled from veterans' trunks in the basement, hemostatic dressing raided from bathroom cabinets, boxes of surgical gloves found under suburban sinks. The various packaged field rations and wool socks went to the side for future sorting; they wouldn't fit into a first-aid kit, but Pax knew they'd serve purpose on the front. Under a sea of plastic-wrapped airway tubes, he found five ballistic chest plates of body armor.

That's one way, Pax thought. He figured more than a few shipping laws had been broken to get the plates here. He stacked them upon the table and cut open the next box.

An hour passed, then another. Lacquered in sweat and feeling a yank in his back, he took a break and unwrapped a cereal bar he'd tucked away that morning. He held up the bottom of his layered shirts so the fan could blast against his bare belly and chest. More than a dozen empty boxes lay under the table. Dozens more loomed ready for unpacking.

He was beginning to count out just how many when a voice said from behind him, "Creative."

It was Yeva. She handed him a bottled water.

"I have a favor to ask."

"No, Yeva, I'm sorry, I won't kill any more puppies for you. Or kittens, or even baby elephants. A man must have a code."

She ignored the bait. "You said you work with cars."

"Yes."

"I am trying to buy a van for Nove Zavtra. Someone is bringing one later, here. Would you look at it, see if it is in the correct shape?"

"Course," Pax said. "Too easy."

"You are a good man, Mister Graves."

The nickname was beginning to bother him. "You're not sure what to make of me, are you?" he said.

Yeva considered that. "Svita is a grown woman. She can do what she wants." She crinkled her brow and looked him up and down. "Many foreigners come and go from Lviv these days. Americans, the most. I protect my friend because she is my friend. And because I was the one to welcome her home when she returned from Milan."

"That—" Pax let his shirts drop and turned away from the fan. He squared himself to face Yeva direct. "She hit me. I was being awful but she hit me. And she's not a small person."

He took a deep breath. He didn't want to talk about this. He didn't like thinking about this. "I get you're protecting her, I respect it, but could you also tell me what to do with all these freaking blankets?"

Yeva refused to glance away. He broke first, pointing to the table with the ballistic plates.

"Those, too."

Yeva waited until he looked back. "Swallowing our pride is never easy, and I think the world makes that harder for men," she finally said. "Yes, follow me, the blankets have their own spot."

"And the plates?"

"I'll send someone," she said.

Over lunch of cold soup and sandwiches, Pax met another American volunteer named Trent. Trent said he was ex–Delta Force, a sniper, at that. That seemed unlikely to Pax—any commandos he'd met tended not to introduce themselves as one—but he did sport a gnarly neck scar that could've well come from an ISIS fighter in Syria, as claimed. He was muscular and twitchy, unable to stay still, eyes roving the corners and doors of the warehouse. He was also the first Black person Pax had seen over here. When he learned Pax had fought in Afghanistan, his voice thinned to a conspiratorial pitch.

"You know I was just in Mariupol."

"No kidding," Pax said.

They'd been shelled for weeks, Trent said, his squad barely managing to sneak through the Russian lines. "Thank Christ the orcs have no night vision."

The artillery had been constant, "rolling fucking barrages," Trent went on. The Russians were shit at urban movement but they had numbers and kept on coming. "Any foreign fighter still there keeps one bullet for themselves. Just in case." The pupils in his eyes glowed like hot coal, then refracted. "There's a propaganda war beyond the battlefield. Putin will nut himself the day they capture an American alive."

Pax nodded solemnly. He was speaking with a lunatic, he felt sure of it. Not that he could condemn much but it was a matter of degrees. "It's good you're here now," he said, "still helping out."

"I'm going back in a couple weeks. Soon as I get some affairs in order." Absolute disgust burst from the self-avowed commando. "Hollywood actresses are in Lviv, celebrity chefs, motherfucking *journalists*."

Maybe he is legit, Pax thought. How the hell would I know, either way?

Should I be embarrassed about being here? he then asked himself. Lee's out there, doing what a soldier's supposed to.

I'm here unpacking mail. Important, sure. But it's also something anybody can do.

But I can't, he thought again. Even the thought of going east overheated his mind. I fucking can't. It's like what Roman told his family. I'd be nothing but a burden.

He had more in common with the youngest Boyko son than anyone else he'd met in Ukraine. That realization brought on the shame the other man in the warehouse felt simply for being in Lviv.

Trent said he had a meeting with like-minded souls to get to, though his attention had drifted upward to the warehouse's observation deck, where Yeva stood conversing with a dumpy, middle-aged man in a leather jacket. "Watch your six, light fighter," Trent said. Then he was gone.

Yeva walked down the metal stairs with the man, signaling to Pax to follow them outside. Skin folds drooped down the man's forehead like a hound's, and his mouth was covered by a surgical face mask. Wisps of gray hair shot from the thin camo bandana wrapped around his skull, and he passed by without acknowledgment. The words "BRAVE DREAM" screamed across the back of the man's jacket. Pax followed them into the day.

A white cargo van waited in the lot, parked perpendicular across three spots. The man began walking Yeva around the exterior of it. Pax checked the tread of the tires first, then the headlights. Under the hood he squeezed the hoses and tugged the belts. The coolant was lower than he'd want but nothing alarming. The transmission fluid proved a dark, rusty color, though, which he didn't like, the dipstick carrying a faint scent of burnt toast. He crawled under the van. The CV joints on the axles appeared fine and he noticed no dents and nothing was pooling. At the van's back the exhaust grime was sooty, which was okay, but also a bit oily. Then the VIN on the title didn't match the one on the dashboard. Was that normal over here? Fucking unlikely, he thought. He got behind the wheel and drove the van around the lot. It cycled through all its gears but with small, peculiar tugs.

"Something's up with the transmission," he told Yeva. "I'd want some time with it in a garage to really figure out what's going on, could just need to be flushed, or could be something major." She nodded. The dumpy man made a scratching sound with his throat. "And only eighty thousand kilometers on a fifteen-year-old van? I don't know." He paused, then gave it to her straight. "The VIN's screwy, too. Something's off."

"Thank you, Mister Graves. That is all I need."

"Can I ask how much he's asking?"

"Too much. Thank you, again."

As Pax turned away, he looked over to the man. Below the surgical mask, heavy veins in his neck were throbbing. And there was a patch on the man's jacket shoulder. It displayed the silhouette of a dog, a shepherd with pointy ears and bared teeth.

I should stay, Pax thought, and while he wanted to, nothing about Yeva's demeanor allowed for it. He returned to the warehouse.

Inside, Pax saw Andrei and Unknown sitting together, finishing lunch. He approached and asked if he could join.

"Please, how is your day?" Andrei said, pulling over another folding chair. "Have you won the war?"

"Hah. Unpacked some body armor. That happen a lot?"

"More and more." Andrei's focus seemed elsewhere.

"Hey, who's Yeva with, out back?" They could just make out the tops of their profiles through a far window. The man seemed to be talking to Yeva with a fat thumb wagging about, though it was hard to be sure through the condensation.

"He goes by 'Dog.'" Andrei spoke with a blandness so measured it pricked. "An owner of many successful businesses who started his own volunteer battalion to fight in the Donbas in 2014. He says he is a colonel but no one uses that. Not even his soldiers."

Pax didn't need to ask about the epithet. Dog looked

like an inkblot in human form through the blurry window, hunching his shoulders forward in a way that accentuated his round form.

"I met one of them," he said. "National Idea."

"Many of his people are trapped in Mariupol. The Dog Battalion is very brave." Class guilt, Pax thought, was practically dripping from Andrei. "But is it a terrible thing to say?" He groaned. "I hope they fight to the last man."

A long minute passed in silence. Someone on the ground floor shouted in Ukrainian. "Lunch is over," Andrei said. "Back to work."

Unknown leaned over from his chair as he rose, using Pax's body to help push himself vertical. The man's palm enveloped Pax's entire shoulder and collarbone, and Pax couldn't help but relent under the other man's weight.

"Evil," the giant said, his English plain as day. He was looking out, toward the far window and Dog. "He is evil man."

———

Yeva had mentioned Milan. But Pax was not going to stew, he would not allow it. So on the street tram he fixed his mind on another, earlier memory. He thought again of Capri, and remembered.

It had been their last trip before deployment. Had he

been nervous? He must've been. Casualty reports all over Afghanistan were spiking, a predictable result, the officers said, given the nature of counterinsurgency, but of course, it usually wasn't officers in the casualty reports.

Svitlana had been great that weekend. He recalled that, clear as a reflection. She'd known just when to let him be, slipping away to a gift shop for those conch shell earrings, and she'd known just when to be there so he could blather away about the platoon, about who was squared away and who was a soup sandwich, about who he'd trust in combat and who he was wary of, and whether he could trust himself in the same awaiting crucible.

The island had been nothing but walls of rain. But they'd made do. They had their villa. They had the wine and oysters and strange Spaghetti Western movies neither of them could understand. They had each other's needs and lusts and excesses and limitations, and they'd made do.

She'd asked that weekend about his family. Which was curious, she'd mostly left the subject alone. "Nothing to tell," he'd told her, because he didn't believe there was. He'd also liked being, for her, the man from nowhere.

He smiled in his thoughts. Dusk was rolling in like a wave. An older woman on the tram said hello. Had it happened the way he remembered? Close enough, he decided. It happened

close enough and close enough has to be good enough if anything's ever going to be enough.

"You'll wait?"

He'd asked in the pale still of first light, her straw, black
hair across his bare chest, rain falling over the villa roof and
windows and beyond it only the smells of the island and sea.

"Tomorrow to forever," she'd said. She'd been twenty years
old. He, twenty-three. "You make me feel good, Luke, and
you make me feel safe."

A moment of conviction, no matter what came next.

"Forever, then."

———

He met Svitlana and her son near sunset at the Monument to
the War Glory of the Soviet Army. When he arrived he found
no statues, only a granite foundation with an inscription: "To
the Vanquishers of Nazism." The monument itself, Svitlana
explained, had been dismantled the year prior. Denys wore a
hoodie of a local soccer club, Karpaty, a golden lion standing
against a shield of green and white.

"Soccer's big here, huh?" Pax said, thinking of the man
from the east at the train station.

"They're not even my favorite team," the boy said. "My
dad cheers for them."

The day's wind had settled into a mellow wane. As they walked through a district of old villas and newer concrete-paneled apartment blocks, Denys listed the entire Ukrainian Premier League for his new audience. Brass tridents hung from Svitlana's earlobes, Pax saw, not the conch shells. She reached over and tugged at one of Pax's sideburns.

"You need a haircut," she said.

"You still in that game?"

"It's been a while, I'll admit," she said. She'd worked part-time as a hairdresser in Italy for spending money. "And you?" She cocked an eyebrow. "All that hair in the back, not so much up top . . ."

"I'm just glad to have anything left."

He hadn't meant it as a dig at her bald husband, though he didn't mind when he realized it could be taken as one.

They were approaching a lane of businesses. Church bells began ringing in sequence, an appeal of the sublime to the secular gods of NATO for a no-fly zone. Together they paused under the bell tower of a modest Orthodox church, listening to its chimes. Three sea-green domes topped the building, corroded and hypnotic, a lean cross rising into the sky like a buoy. Pax watched the boy cross himself and Svitlana do the same, and he thought, huh, I don't remember her being religious at all. He bowed his head and closed his eyes all the same.

Hey, You, cloud genie, Pax prayed. If You're up there and bothering to pay attention there's a lot of bad shit happening down here and it'd be cool if You intervened for once. I know that's not Your jam or something because of free will and shit but no one here asked for this war so send Your angel of death to take the one man responsible for all this suffering and ruin, that's the move, dude, don't be a bitch, amen.

At the chocolate house Pax insisted on paying for their pastries and hot cocoas. They sat in the café while Denys watched tempered chocolate get poured into molds through a window.

"Did you know some people at the dinner thought I tossed a puppy off a cliff?" Pax popped his tongue off the roof of his mouth. "I don't even look like that guy."

"I heard about it later." Svitlana rolled her eyes. "I've tried to tell you, ignore them! Some people in Europe think disliking Americans is a personality trait."

Pax smirked and took a large bite of pastry. As he chewed he noticed Denys shuffling his way through the crowd of other kids with a strange hesitance. He wasn't going to comment but Svitlana saw him watching.

"He has macular degeneration. It's genetic, they say. Both parents must carry the recessive gene. It's why he looks at things from the sides of his eyes. It's how he sees."

"Jesus. Is there treatment or anything?"

"Not at this time." A mechanical remoteness filled her voice. This was not the first time she'd had this conversation, nor said these words. "It's why we send him to the international school. They are more understanding with his learning."

"That's good."

"It'll continue to worsen. He may be fully blind by the time he's an adult."

"What about braille?"

"He's resistant. But of course we try." She took a long sip from her cocoa. "I try. Taras ignores it, thinks it'll go away. Like some magic trick. The disabled are considered burdens in Ukrainian society. That his son is not perfect feels a violation. It's all about him, of course."

She has poise now, Pax thought, seeing her temples flex, watching her jawline set with each new divulgence. He'd come here for a young woman he thought he'd once maybe loved and found a grown person he wanted desperately to be worthy of.

I'm here to help, he wanted to tell her. Please let me help.

"If we don't leave this country," she continued, "the war will take Denys one way or another. Already he asks how he can shoot a gun at Russians with his eyes. An entire generation of children will forever have them as the enemy, and they'll be right to. This war will not be a short one. He will grow up in it. They all will.

"And I thank God many times a day he will not fight. As his mother, this is the most normal thing in the world. The army will not come for him. But I see the hurt, the pain on him, as he begins to realize this. And I know the only way to save him from that is to take him far from his country and let him be anything but Ukrainian."

Pax looked across the table. He reached across for her hand. She hesitated but let him.

There were no second chances. He believed that, knew it to be true. Just get to tomorrow, that was the whole thing. Life dangled dreams in front of people as a bright cloak, only to snatch it away if you dared try to reach them. Pax knew this, he'd figured out the score and told himself never again, no more, more times than he could count. But maybe, Pax thought again. Perhaps this was something else.

She stretched out a finger and began twirling, with a long, orange nail, a prayer bead on his wrist.

"You changed over there. Didn't you?"

"Lana." She was still twirling the bead. "There's something I should tell you about that. What I said the other night—"

"Me first." Her finger stopped but her hand stayed, her eyes holding a steady calm. "Milan was my fault. I handled it, everything, poorly. You needed me to be a rock. A problem was, I needed one, too. I had already come back here, was building a life. I knew it was a mistake to go. But you were so insisting. And I did miss you."

Pax heard a noise repeating and repeating and realized it was his knee shaking against the underside of the table. He tucked in his leg so it could no longer reach and said, "I wanted things to be like they had been." He thought about that. "Which was stupid."

"You were alone," she said. She squeezed his hand. "I know that was hard."

Old hurt tore through his chest like wildfire. He'd buried so much of his life from then deep away, not on purpose, but to survive, to be able to just get to tomorrow. His mid-tour leave, in particular—it felt like something had split clean there, between before and after, rising and falling, and in the middle of it all lay only Svitlana Dovbush and her trident tattoo, tangled in bedsheets in a damp, haughty city surrounded by mountains.

Then Pax had returned to Afghanistan. The suicide bomber attacked the checkpoint a week after he got back. Seven days, exactly.

Had he been thinking about Svitlana, and Milan, and what had gone wrong between them, in that gunner's cupola? Must've been, he thought. I must've been. It's all I could think about. It was impossible for him to separate any of it, even when he knew he should, it had all braided together in the decade since. In the café, Pax heard another noise, repeating. It was his own pulse, hammering away in the pit of his neck.

"We had fun. Didn't we?" Wistfulness laced Svitlana's words. No, Pax thought, no. Not again.

"I'll take you all," he said. His voice was rushed but firm. "To Europe, Barcelona, whatever. To America, if you want. We can get away."

Svitlana frowned and shook her head. "No, Luke. I could do that myself if I decided to. I am not helpless. But there's nothing to be done." She took back her hand. "Despite everything, we must wait. It's all we can do. A boy needs a father." She looked away. "He needs *his* father."

Another air-raid siren howled down from the holy above, abolishing whatever was supposed to come next.

VI

As a young boot, Han Lee had learned the only time a soldier could be alone, really alone, was Sunday morning, early, reveille hour, before there were any traces of light, before the surprise inspections and work details and the chaplain, when life was still pitch-black and boundless. A man could think then. He could evaluate, and assess, and plan. And a soldier with a plan could never be surprised by the bullshit of tomorrow. So Lee had developed a habit: no matter where he was, whether coming off a grueling combat patrol on the far edge of the world or fifteen-beers-deep in garrison, wallowing in stripper dust and regret, Sunday morning, 5:00 a.m., he found a corner by himself and cleaned his weapon. Then, only then, could he think about the week to his immediate front.

He'd turned astray in civilian life, gone soft from the comforts. Sleeping off the hangovers seemed natural enough but it had led to no thinking, and then no planning, and then no purpose. In this way, Ukraine offered a way of return. It offered it in so much else, too. The least he could do was set a fucking alarm.

The barracks at Yavoriv were newer and shinier than anything Lee had slept in while in Uncle Sam's army. Same with the dining facility. And the command building. Which he found funny. If the American taxpayers only knew, he thought, finding a table in the empty courtyard. He set down the solvent and rags and rifle. If those jabroni fucksticks only knew.

There were no stars out. Just infinite dark.

Ahh, they don't want to know. He answered his own rhetorical question. They pay to keep ignorant. Same as it's ever been. That's the whole puppet show.

Before he'd been sent to Italy, he'd served in Hawaii, a baby-faced private with a slavish devotion to the vast new order that'd accepted him into its ranks. Now those were some old-ass barracks, he remembered. Preserved way too long because they'd been strafed by Japanese fighter planes coming through Kolekole Pass on their way to Pearl Harbor, creating a historic landmark in the process.

A real war, Lee thought. One that mattered.

Lee had been some places and seen some things. He took pride in this. He'd become the man he'd wanted to be as a boy, almost. Now he was here, in a country he couldn't have found on a globe a month prior, to complete his one outstanding task.

I'm not the killer man. He hummed the old cadence to himself. *I'm the killer man's son. But I'll do the killing till the killer man comes.*

He disassembled his weapon to rub it down piecemeal, flashlight between his teeth to not misplace the bolt carrier or firing pin. The Ukrainians had tried issuing them rusty AK-47s left over from the Cold War. No bueno, Lee and the others had told them. We'll fight for you but you gotta outfit us right. Behold, a third party soon arrived with a truckful of standard-issue NATO weaponry and ballistic plates, factory-fresh and lacking any serial numbers. Praise be.

He'd known as soon as the first Drago tanks crossed the border he was coming here. It'd been haunting him before he left, like an itch he couldn't reach, a nightmare he couldn't shake. He didn't know why but he knew he'd never be content, never fully realized, if he didn't come and fight and do something that was all right and all good and all true.

We don't get to choose our wars, he'd told Paxton. And he'd meant it. Because this one had chosen him.

Did he miss his girls? Sure. This was how he'd become the man they needed him to be, though. How he'd set the example.

By killing another man? Lee's conscience, or the voice beneath it, sometimes probed with hippie questions like this. Which was good. It kept him honest.

No. By killing a killer.

Ukraine held the world's gaze. He was in the midst of it now. He'd walked the periphery of history before but this was its center. While others hung blue-and-yellow flags on their porches or posted messages of solidarity to Twitter or told their girlfriends how much they wanted to come over, *if only*, he was here, he'd fucking come. He was the man of action. He was the motherfucking Yellow Reb. Hundreds like him had come, too, Brits, Frenchies, Baltics, even a goddamn Peruvian. Maybe not the thousands-strong the government was proclaiming but that was okay. Being a soldier meant being a political prop, Lee knew the deal. Just how it was.

He reassembled his rifle. It smelled right now, correct, not metallic and stiff but oily and lethal.

Not everyone at Yavoriv was proving to be who they said they were. Today's focus would be fire and maneuver, basic stuff but the bedrock of foot-soldiering. They still needed more interpreters but the translation barriers could be over-come. Lee led from the front. He knew how to communicate with force.

His watch charted through the black: 5:45 a.m. The chow hall opened in fifteen minutes. He hadn't taken to local cui-sine but it was hard to fuck up sausage and eggs.

He heard a shrill whine through the vastness above. It sounded like a falling man, or an angry machine. As Lee looked up, the sky bloomed bright like an enormous flower, redder than any sun he'd ever known. Then he blinked, and it was gone.

———————

Pax whirled through the doors of the coffeehouse, his mind a million places with a million different possibilities. Anything seemed plausible except what was most likely. He saw Merri-man at a table along the front window.

"What have you heard? What do you know?"

The other man stared at him, eyes bloodshot behind hip-ster frames, his wide mouth curling around empty air for an answer. He held a chewed pen in his hand and scratched his scalp with it.

"Not much more than what's been reported. A couple dozen cruise missiles from long-range bombers. Targeted the new command center but struck a bunch else. Officially they're saying thirty killed, maybe a hundred wounded."

"Unofficially?"

Merriman's eyebrows sharpened to darts.

"I've been told one could conservatively triple both tallies."

Pax looked away, into the guts of the coffeehouse. It was Viennese style, with red curtains and chandeliers and grandfather-clock authority, a remainder of a forgotten empire that had once claimed this city as an outpost. Then it had lost a war and another empire had moved in, albeit one that also enjoyed espresso and pastries in the morning. Then it all happened again. Had the Poles come before or after the Austro-Hungarians? Pax couldn't recall. Both preceded the Nazis, he was sure of it, who in turn gave way to the Soviets, he was sure of that, too. But before them . . . he couldn't remember the precise order, but he kept trying to. For once he didn't mind the fixed past where hard answers lay, even if he himself didn't know them. If he could stay there, somehow, and unsort the order of dominion, somehow, maybe the present would settle, as well.

"I'm sure you've tried." His former captain dragged him back to the moment. "But his number won't connect."

"I'm fucking aware of that, J.T."

The other man did not react to the use of his first name.

He simply blinked and nodded. "We'll get clarity, Paxton. I promise you I'm working every contact I can."

The sirens had begun wailing around dawn. Pax stayed in bed through them. Then his phone started pinging. Texts and calls and messages asking if he was safe, had he been there, did he know anyone who had? More Black Sea strikes, he thought through the somnolence. Maybe another firefight at Chernobyl. People over there kept thinking Ukraine was some single thing, a little quaint place at the end of a long road, not a gigantic nation as big and sprawling as Texas. Then he'd seen the note from Lee's ex-wife, a person he'd met only once in Italy a decade before, and a dark chill ripped him awake.

"Are you and Han ok?" it read. "News is talking about missiles and the base at Yavoriv. It's got us worried."

He still hadn't replied to her. He didn't know how to.

"The Ukrainians said he was fine." Pax wasn't speaking to Merriman so much as he was giving audience to an insistence in his head. "Said he was with the right people."

"Yeah. Well." Merriman took off his glasses and rubbed at his eyes and for only the second time since Pax had known him, the man's endless certainty seemed to crack. "They know more than we do, but that doesn't mean it's much."

The sky, of course it was the goddamn sky, Pax thought. I knew it as soon as we got here, something's wrong up there, we can't see, can't know, it's too bleak, too gray, even on clear days no one can see anything. In Afghanistan the locals had called the American drones buzzbuzzaks. This was like that but on steroids. And we laughed about their dread, Pax thought. It's awful but it's true because we controlled the sky and couldn't even conceive not, and we laughed when they started clucking over engine noises and contrails, because we knew when there'd be Hellfire rain and we wouldn't be there for it. We thought we were little gods.

A failure of imagination then. A failure of imagination now.

Pax couldn't sit still. He got up and began wrapping his hands around the back of his chair. "Who in their goddamn mind put them all together?" He needed someone to blame. "The same base that NATO built. Are they fucking retarded?"

Merriman just looked at him.

"This is why there needs to be a no-fly zone. Fucking Biden. Fucking Boris Johnson."

"An NFZ wouldn't have mattered here." Merriman's certitude was back. "Those bombers never left Russian airspace."

"So it was inevitable?" Pax was trying not to hyperventilate. He reached for Merriman's glass of water but set it back down because it was empty. "That's what you're telling me?"

"Maybe he was bunking somewhere else. Maybe he's already been sent to Kyiv. Maybe he's pulling bodies from wreckage as we speak. You've got to calm down." Merriman put his glasses back on. "And lower your voice." His own dropped to a whisper. "Ears are everywhere, man. City's crawling with saboteurs."

It was the "man" that riled Pax more than anything. His former commander was feigning at amity, playacting at a rapport they'd never had and never would. Lower his voice? Fuck that fucking noise. His friend, his sergeant, was possibly dead less than an hour from them and this guy was saying they couldn't go and look, couldn't even try, all they could do was wait for info from some mysterious source, because why, exactly, had Merriman even said what he was doing over here, said who he was with, in what capacity? Pax knew who he'd been in Wardak. A motherfucking fraud, that was who, a goddamn poser, the kind of officer who expected others to get their hands dirty while he stayed far away and pristine. And by the way, did he even think about Private First Class Shiloh anymore, how he, as the commander, was responsible for that kid's deletion from existence? You ordered me not to shoot and I could have, Pax said, shouted really, he was crying, trying to breathe, trying to find anything like a center while he gripped the back of his chair tighter and tighter, you ordered me to hold my fire, and I could have saved them, could have stopped that car bomb if only you hadn't opened your fucking mouth, and they're gone, not just Shiloh, but the others, as well, Rivers sucked off a shotgun, Jimenez lived in trap houses, no one even knew what'd happened to Antone, anyone at that checkpoint was now fucked-up or dead, a lost squad of hard-chargers ruined for no goddamn reason, all because Captain Jordan Todd "J.T." Merriman Jr., U.S. Army, infantry, commanding, had ordered him to stand down, and he, Corporal Luke Paxton, not-commanding, had made the fatal fucking mistake of listening. And now it'd happened again except there were no remains to scoop this time, missiles didn't leave anything like that, and while Pax didn't know much about Yavoriv or Ukraine or the military-industrial complex or much else for that matter, his face smearing hot with tears and snot, he did know that J.T. fucking Merriman should never again call him "man," they weren't pals, they weren't buds, so he could kiss his skinny enlisted ass.

A strident pause followed. Pax focused, as much as he could, on his breathing.

"Feel better?" Even in equanimity, Merriman couldn't help but condescend. Pax refused the other man's offer of a napkin and wiped his face with the sleeves of his jacket. He looked around the coffeehouse. The vigilant glances of onlookers dove like birds. A young boy across the way kept on him, though. He was about Denys's age, chunkier, affixed with a rabid focus. I'm the crazy person, Pax thought. The ugly American. But then he remembered Lee, and being the disturbed foreigner mattered much less.

Merriman told him to sit. Pax said he preferred to stand.

"Why I'm here." The other man rasped his words, spitting them out like seed shells caught on his lips. "I'm helping stand up their territorial defense, make it more than names on a list. I'm coordinating logistical runs for Ukrainian SOF. Fuel's the most critical need out there right now. I'm sure a wise, macro-thinker such as yourself already knows that. I'm helping establish an underground railroad to evac civilians and wounded internationals. It's true, my main priority at this second isn't Yavoriv. One of my guys has been driving orphans and pregnant women out of the south but we haven't heard from him in seventy-two hours. I'm damn worried.

"These are real, practical ways to contribute, Paxton. I'm not the one staggering around this city like a beggar asking to be handed a purpose."

Pax tried to interject. Playing the orphans card was unfair and he intended to say so. But his former captain was not done.

"Afghanistan. Not a day goes by that I don't think about Shiloh and everyone else at that checkpoint. Even if I didn't want to I'd feel it from the metal balls still in my hip. As I recall, you were the only one there not physically hurt. And hey, I know about trauma and moral injury. But come on. You should consider how lucky you were, sometime, not how cheated you were.

"Twelve Afghans were killed at that checkpoint, too, Paxton. It's interesting you never seem to bring them up. You ever give one thought to them? I have. If you need some burden lifted, yes, it's true, I ordered you not to shoot because I was thinking about those civilians around us. I decided in that moment we were the soldiers, we'd volunteered to incur risk. They hadn't. It was the wrong call and it torments me every minute, every day. But don't you dare fucking presume I don't think about them, that I don't remember them. They're why I'm here now.

"Now get the fuck out of my sight. I have work to do."

Pax had been dismissed. There was no other way to put it. Merriman was the forever commander; he, a forever grunt. He hated Merriman for this and he hated himself even more as he complied, it made him feel low and low-class. Yet he still did it. As he departed the coffeehouse, artwork about Putin's height greeted him, then brittle air and church bells.

————

He was due at the warehouse at noon. Andrei and Unknown needed help unloading a large shipment of heavy-duty shovels. Getting the shovels to the front was important. Trenches didn't dig themselves. And Yeva wanted him to look at another van. This one was supposed to be, Dog had assured her, in fine condition.

Pax didn't want to go, reasoned that he shouldn't, told himself he wasn't in the right frame of mind, that he'd be checking his phone too frantically to be of any use. So he returned to the flat. He opened a box of red wine Andrei had procured for him. There were four bottles in it and he didn't bother with a glass.

As he drank, he tried to think. He was still charged from the encounter with Merriman. He thumbed his prayer beads wrapped around his wrist and thought of all the things he should've said in the coffeehouse, that he could've said if only he'd known to. Fucking Merriman had ambushed him. He texted Lee again. He wrote him on Facebook, and Instagram, as well. He reread the message from Lee's ex-wife but did not reply to it.

Had he thought about the Afghans from the checkpoint? Of course he had. Fucking Merriman. He remembered the exact pitch of that old woman's screams, they'd been what sent him to the VA in the first place. He'd been the one who . . . the motherfucker had ambushed him.

He'd forgotten Merriman had been wounded. It was surprising to learn shrapnel remained in the man's hip. Maybe sometimes he did think about Shiloh and the others. Maybe he would take it back if he could.

No, Pax thought. Don't do that. It's just another way for him to get ahead, to leverage that day into personal gain. I bet he tells the story at business luncheons. He got mad because I called him out. "Ears are everywhere, man." Shut the fuck up, man.

Pax finished the bottle and went to open another. He told himself to slow down. Only a little more, he thought. He was almost calm now, he could feel it. Only a little more.

Lee still hadn't replied. As far as Pax could tell, nothing he'd sent had been read. Which makes sense, Pax thought. The mobile towers and shit. He's pulling bodies from the wreckage. That's something he'd be doing, for sure.

On his phone, Pax found a news article about the missile strike, posted ten minutes before. It talked about multiple buildings destroyed and the craters found in the aftermath, as deep and scattered as the ones on the moon. A government spokesman in Kyiv said only Ukrainian soldiers had been killed or injured, which sent a rush through Pax's body. But an anonymous Russian official was quoted at the end of the article. "We delivered 180 foreign mercenaries to hell this morning," it read. "This is a dispute between cousins. Any

Western outsiders who interfere with our special military operation will meet this fate."

Pax texted Merriman the article. A bubble with three dots appeared. Pax waited. Then the bubble disappeared. It seemed the other man had decided not to respond.

Near the bottom of the second bottle, Pax remembered he had a date that evening. Well, not a date, a haircut, but yesterday, before the missiles and Yavoriv and everything else, he'd hoped and believed it could turn into a date. Lovely, he thought. I'm drunk. He took a shower to try to sober up, then drank multiple glasses of water from the sink. There was a flat, metallic taste but it settled into his stomach. He thought about this. It'd been less than two weeks since Lee had told him about the old pipes of Lviv.

"How?" Pax asked the empty flat. "Why?" He hurried out the door.

Drunken thoughts came to Pax like flitting bats while he was on the tram. Lee crowing through the flat: "Wake up, son! Glory to the motherfucking heroes." Bogdan's joke at the dinner party: "A Russian rifleman, tanker, and pilot are returning to Moscow from the front. Who is driving?" Yeva in the warehouse telling him he'd been confused for a puppy murderer. There were still no replies from Lee or Merriman or anyone else and he sat with his head against the window, a crushing sense of loneliness plunging through him. Tears welled in the pits of his eyes.

Pull it together, he thought. Don't be like this.

He'd meant to bring a gift for Denys, a Nerf gun or large-print book, something he remembered only as he turned onto Mykhaylivskyy Street. He walked an imaginary line along the road as if on a field-sobriety test. Svitlana answered the door wearing a long, black barber smock.

"Sorry I'm late," he said. "Gypsy."

He tried to move into the house but she put an arm out, across the entry. She peered into his face as if it were a wishing well.

"Have you been crying?"

She bore dark eye shadow and big hoop earrings made of tarnished metal and colored glass. We have no time, Pax thought. It felt like realization and reason at once, death comes for us all, the cruelest part is that we don't know when, sometimes it eats us slow and methodical from the inside like cancer, other times it comes out of the sky like a fucking missile, and he needed to share this epiphany with Svitlana, because she was here and he was here and who knew how long that would be true, no one, that was the whole damn thing of it, to live, to die, to remember, and he thought about what Lee had told him about being a doer, and he wanted to be like that, a person of action, or at least someone who tried.

He told her as much as he could. About Lee, about Yavoriv, about time and fate and mortality. It came out jumbled.

"Luke, are you okay?"

"Do you remember?" he asked, trying again. "Do you ever wonder what if?"

"Are you hearing me, Luke?"

He cupped her chin and leaned in and kissed her.

She kissed back, at first, her tongue sliding into his mouth with an old ease. He moved his hand to the shallow of her back and pulled her closer. He smelled traces of her shampoo and tasted the balm of her chapstick. But then she recoiled and wrenched away. She stepped back from him and into her home.

"No," she said. "No."

"Why?"

"I don't know who you are."

He staggered from the closed door. I shouldn't be surprised, he thought. Yet I am. He could still taste her chapstick and it filled him with tremendous longing. He felt tears again running his vision.

He found a wine bottle in the depths of his coat. He hadn't remembered putting it there but he had, there it was. He twisted it open. He wanted to be apart, alone, away from war-torn faces and old-world judgment and messy, unknowable questions. He moved to an isolated stretch of concrete along the fence line of the cemetery. Falling vestiges of sun bled west against the hush of dusk. Wind gusts swept through the air and wagged at Pax's cheeks and tunneled down his neck, into his chest and core.

Many thoughts were grappling and groaning at him but he denied all comers. A man of action, he thought, and he drank from the bottle of wine.

He walked by a large warp in the fence. A few steps later he turned around and entered the cemetery through it. Shaggy forest cleaved by sloping paths crammed the distance. He noticed a midnight-blue bird on a bush. He looked it dead in the eye. It just watched him pass.

There were sculpture gardens and stone angels and vast fields of crosses. He saw people picnicking at a grave under a tree. He shouted gibberish at them. They either didn't understand or pretended not to. Different sections of graves were devoted to different things, a hill of rebels, a failed uprising, child soldiers, victims of secret police. A kindled flame signaled entry to the burial ground for the fallen of the Great Patriotic War, which is a funny name, Pax thought, when you think about it. He was tired and thirsty so he found a gnarled tree with a base clean of mud and undergrowth and leaned down against it. He drank more wine and promptly fell asleep.

———————

Svitlana locked the door and watched Luke through a sheer curtain at her window. He was crying again and mumbling to himself. He lurched away down the street. After she decided he would not return, she took off her barber smock and hung it in the hallway closet. Somewhere back there, she knew, behind her shoe racks and a bin of Denys's outgrown gloves and winter hats, was a wooden jewelry box with her engagement and wedding rings in it. Then she walked to the kitchen, poured herself a stiff glass of chardonnay, and took a seat at the counter.

She was upset with Luke. She was upset with herself. Had she led him on in some way? Of course, she thought. You knew what you were doing. Men are simple creatures and you've known that since you were young. You've enjoyed seeing him. You've enjoyed being appreciated.

Yet how dare he. She wondered about the friend he mentioned, the one he thought had been at Yavoriv. The news from there was terrible. Then she thought: yes, it had been nice, in its way, being held by a man again, being kissed, even by one who smelled so much of wine.

A moment from the past flashed into her mind, the two of them on a trip, Jesolo, perhaps, watching a cowboy movie, dubbing it with silly dialogue themselves because neither could understand Italian, and laughing, laughing so much, laughing to laugh. There had been wine, and oysters, and so much laughter. It was hard to reconcile that Luke Paxton with this one. There'd been a fresh innocence to him on all their trips, seeing old Mediterranean cities and ruins with genuine wonder. He'd always told her he was no one, from nowhere. Whatever you could say about Italy, she remembered, it was absolutely and utterly somewhere.

These thoughts were making her sentimental, she felt it in her chest. So Svitlana did what she often did when the visceral pricked at her. She counteracted a good memory with a bad one. Luke kept insisting on bringing up Milan. "Well I was there, too," she said out loud in her kitchen. "I remember, too."

When he left for Afghanistan, she'd come home to Lviv. They'd agreed they were too young. They'd agreed not to take things too seriously. They'd agreed the distance was too much and that the future was so open, but they'd keep in touch. And they did. He'd written her as often as he could from Wardak, and she didn't know what to do with it, or him. He needed her in a way he never had when they'd been together. And then he'd begged her to meet him in Milan, and begged her, and begged her.

Was that why she'd gone? Be honest with yourself, at least, she thought. She'd gone because all her friends in Lviv were playing musical chairs, settling down with partners they'd known since childhood. She'd decided to ignore the melody. Whatever it was I was seeking back then, Svitlana thought, it was more than a wedding.

He'd met her at the Milan train station. He'd landed that morning and looked—well, he'd looked like he'd been in an internment camp. He was pale and bug-eyed and had lost twenty pounds of muscle and jittered with wild, nervous energy, like some stereotype of a veteran in an American war movie, but of course she couldn't say that. Then he'd kissed her, and it felt right, and she'd said she was happy to see him, because she was.

Had it happened the way she was remembering? It must have, she thought. Whatever lapses there were didn't matter. The essence remained, pure as light.

He'd been fine at dinner. Aloof but fine. She'd mentioned she'd found a new rental in Lviv, a deal courtesy of a family friend. He'd asked for the address. She'd written it down in his notebook. After, they'd gone to the hotel and made love. That night she'd woken from a bad dream to find a nightmare. He was drunk, pacing the room half-dressed, looming over the bed holding out her laptop and screaming, "Who is he? Is it that fucking Chmilenko guy? Tell me, show me!"

He'd been trying to hack her Facebook again. "I thought we got past this," she'd said, leaving out that she had been seeing Taras in Lviv, here and there. He was a law student, serious and striving in a way she found attractive. Luke's seriousness, which was war's seriousness, was not something she could contend with.

A dark irony, she thought. As it's now come for us, and I've no choice.

Luke had asked about things he had no right to. When she didn't answer or deny him, he'd called her a bitch. He'd called her a slut. There was a savagery in his movements and voice she didn't know, and didn't trust. So when he went to grab her wrist to pull her vertical she hit him as hard as she could, striking him flush in the cheek.

In her kitchen a decade later, Svitlana could still picture the shock and hurt on his face, and feel the shock and hurt in her hand.

"We're done," she'd said, "forever," and he'd left the room, not unlike the way he'd just left her door. She returned to the train station within the hour. He'd written her messages on

Facebook in the ensuing weeks. She deleted each one without reading. Around the time the messages stopped, Taras asked if she was interested in dating more exclusively.

Do I ever wonder what if? Chewing the tips of her hair, Svitlana considered the question. No. Because life is confusing enough.

The sudden sound of the front door tossing open sent her heart into overdrive. I locked it, she thought, I know I did! She stood and reached for the handle of a bread knife.

"Is dinner ready?"

Denys, she thought. Of course it's my beautiful boy. It would be no one else. She relinquished the handle.

"Sorry, baby. Not yet." She skipped over asking where he'd been. She knew. He and his friend Nazar trekked down to the chocolate house as often as they could. "Have fun?"

There was no answer. As she went to the freezer to cobble together a quick meal, she looked over to her son and found bafflement splayed across his clay face.

"Mom," he said. "Why are you crying?"

The wet and the cold woke Pax. It was absolute dark and beads of rain dripped onto him from the tree. He wasn't sober but he wasn't drunk anymore, and the wine bottle had spilled over at his side. The first cohesive thing his mind latched onto was, "I don't know who you are."

The second thing was the air-raid siren. It sounded both close and far-flung, above him and infernally beneath, a bombardment on his senses. He kept still and pretended to be dead in the cemetery until the siren stopped.

A dim lamppost guided him down to a wide path. Pax found a visitors' map along it and located the nearest exit. A little American flag was stamped on the way there. Fat, cool raindrops fell on him and he tried not to think about his wet clothes or the coldness or how long a walk remained between him and shelter. At the spot the map had marked with the flag he found a creamy marble headstone with a matching sculpture. It depicted a man wearing coveralls and a leather cap with earflaps. He was adorned with angel wings.

"LIEUTENANT EDMUND PIKE GRAVES (1891–1919)," the headstone read. "GOD BLESS AMERICA. POLSKE KOŚCIUSZKO."

Who the hell are you, Pax thought, and how did you get here? The man's Wikipedia page held answers. Pax was halfway through it before realizing this must've been the Mister Graves of Yeva's incessant teasing.

He'd been a pilot, a World War I veteran who'd remained in Europe and volunteered to fight for Poland in some war

Pax had never heard of. His contemporaries described him as a good pilot, a risk-taker, but bona fide, a legitimate hero.

Graves didn't die in combat, though. He crashed his plane during an air show celebrating an anniversary of the city's defense. Which seemed a uniquely pointless way to go out, even for war.

Mister Graves, Mister Graves, Pax thought, the stupid American. I hope they all get a good chuckle from it.

Then he thought, I don't want this. I can't be buried here, forgotten and alone, a peculiarity with a flag sticker. They're wrong about me. They're fucking wrong.

"I fix things," he said out loud. Something sharp and hot swelled in Pax's chest and that spurred him to keep going. "This is a heavy-metals war. A fires war. They may not know it. Neither do you, flyboy," he told the headstone. "But they need me."

He let go of his new grievance on his walk through the old city. Compared to the troubles of the world, what did it matter? She didn't know who he was. Lee still hadn't replied anywhere.

VII

The next-morning apology parade was not new to Pax. First he texted Yeva and Andrei. Then he sent Merriman a note. He deliberated a few minutes over the last one. Finally he typed, "I'm sorry, Lana, for everything. Good luck to you and your son. I'll be rooting for you."

A thousand little drills bored into his brain. He made his way to the shower and tried to piece himself back together. He returned thirty minutes later to zero replies.

When his phone did ping, it wasn't someone he'd expected to hear from.

"Light fighter, this is Trent from the warehouse," the text read. "Came across a thing you might be interested in. Hit me up if u r free."

Why not, Pax thought. Anything's better than stewing here.

An address followed to a sporting-goods store in the southern reaches of the city. It was an hour-plus walk from the flat but Pax didn't mind. It gave him something to do. The rain had stopped and the day was wrapped in a wintry drab. He tried not to stare into the sky too much, not that it relinquished anything when he did. Trent stood waiting outside the shop, squeezed into a navy tee shirt with no jacket, a coyote-brown assault pack on his shoulder.

"There he is." Trent slapped hands with Pax like they'd known one another for years. "You see that shit about Yavoriv?"

Pax said that he had.

Trent introduced two others standing alongside him: Brad, a short man wearing a backward baseball cap, and Paul, a tall man wearing a beanie. They were also American, middle-aged, and both bristled when asked if they were with the legion.

"We're not involved with that." Trent seemed amused. "We're more, like, freelancers."

Pax was too hungover for surreptitiousness. "What's that mean?" he asked.

Brad said he worked in land-mine clearance. Paul described himself as a servant of God.

Pax smiled. He thought it was a joke. It was not.

"This is not your average missionary." Trent's amuse-ment and goodwill fell away, replaced by a procedural sort of hyper-earnestness. "Between us schoolgirls, Paul here is the head of operations of Wheelwright Ministries." When Pax didn't react, the other man continued. "They've done a lot of killing across the globe."

"All in aid of our fellow brothers and sisters in Christ," Paul said.

The man did carry the heedful glaze of a zealot, Pax saw, now that he went looking for it. He treaded forward with care.

"A professional crew," he said. "What you all want with me?"

"Oh. No. We're doing something else." Trent pointed to the store behind him. "More of a connect thing. That guy from the warehouse, Dog? We just met with him. He's look-ing for some folks to do some stuff. I thought of you." The self-avowed Delta sniper winked. "It'll beat sorting through mail deliveries from fucking Middletown, USA, I know that much."

Pax walked where directed, more to get away from the strange, unblinking missionary than anything else. Holy was one thing, he thought. Too holy, another.

The shop seemed closed, its lights off and metal bars low-ered across its window. The front door tugged open. Pax moved into a narrow corridor, three skinhead bruisers with security wands and slung rifles forming a half-moon around him. One grunted at him through an adit of blocky brown teeth and hell breath, holding out a plastic bin. Pax took the cue and placed his phone in it. Another gestured with the snout of his gun to a flight of stairs. Above it, along the lintel, a large, limp flag sagged. It bore a black sun, twelve radial beams splaying out from the core.

"Which floor?"

The bruiser with the hell breath held up three fingers.

He climbed the stairs, either too hungover or too emotionally drained for much caution. And hey, he thought. You only live once.

Which was not something he'd ever said or even thought before. Lee had, though, many times.

He emerged from the stairwell onto a floor lined with beige office carpet and display cases. Dim lighting shined through the space—the near corner held a row of portraits of Cossack warriors on horseback, in front of which rose a pedestal with a large, silver-plated revolver under glass. It's a museum, Pax realized. He moved through the floor with wary curiosity; there were maps of ancient Ukraine and belt buckles with swastikas on them and a pair of full-size tridents made from gold that conjured up Svitlana's earrings and hip tattoo. In the center of the room was a mannequin wearing a modern green military uniform, digital flora–patterned, complete with a helmet and black ski mask. It gripped a long, elegant sniper rifle between its fiberglass hands. As Pax approached it, he heard laughter and coughing coming from an adjacent room. He knocked on the open door.

"Ahh, Yeva Boyko's motor inspector." The man Pax knew as Dog sat on a floral couch in the room. He was watching television and eating ribs. An open Styrofoam box of bones gnawed clean lay between his feet. Dog ripped a chunk of meat from the piece in his hands, then began to suck on one of the ends.

"Best flavor," he said through a series of slurping noises, "always closer to the bone."

He offered a rib to Pax, who demurred. He pointed to a minifridge in the corner. On top of it, the man's surgical face mask was scrunched up in a ball. Courage Juice stocked the fridge itself. Pax accepted one of those, then took a seat in a stained beach chair. Dog muted the television.

"Tell me," he said, picking through his teeth with his tongue. "How do you find the City of Lions?"

"A lot of history." Pax nodded outward. "Some of which you seem to own."

"Zhukov carried that revolver. The Red Army was sixty

percent Ukrainian back then." Dog reached into a pocket for a cigarette and lighter. His skin was gray and stubbled and speckled with liver spots; his mouth, Pax thought, now that he could see it, did not fit his face. It was far too narrow. "This is why they will lose. They do not know how to win without us."

Pax scanned the smaller room. Dog's leather jacket hung from a hook under a pinup of a clothed, virginal calendar girl. Another flag with the superimposed dog logo was framed on the inner wall, this one with the national blue and yellow colors. When he looked back, the militia leader was examining him from under his brow through a thin haze of cigarette smoke.

"Is this why you came to Lviv? For the history?"

The ceaseless question. Pax tried a new answer.

"There's so much I don't understand about this place," he said. "Some things I'm not even sure I like. But as soon as I got here, I knew it as something worth being part of. I don't know if that's why I came. It's why I've stayed."

The other man made a scratching sound with his throat.

"I understand many of your soldiers fight in Mariupol among the rear guard. You must be proud."

Dog took a long drag, then rubbed under his camo bandana with his cigarette hand. More liver spots emerged. He had fat, stubby fingers, the fingers of a man of capital. Something like a response growled through the smoke.

"They fall back to the steel plant. Our own government treats us like beasts to sacrifice. They will become martyrs, but it did not have to be this way."

Pax didn't know what to say to that.

"Betrayed by the same nation we swore ourselves to. And still we stack bodies of the horde. For ourselves, now. For honor."

Pax held to the quiet. Dog made another scratching sound with his throat.

"You know the wife of the lawyer. Yes?"

Pax nodded.

"Chernenko, one of Lviv's favorite sons. He once refused to represent me, but that was many years ago." Dog trilled his lips. "Too bad what happens in Kherson."

"What?" Shock coursed through Pax. "What do you mean?"

Dog shrugged. "His unit, they were overrun. I hold no secret information. He was a better defender in the courtroom, maybe, than in battle."

Again Pax didn't know what to say.

Dog sat up with a start.

"Have you been to the front?"

Pax shook his head.

"Azov mud and snails. They crunch under our boots. Have to use a knife or screwdriver to clean the guts away."

This is the weirdest interview, Pax thought. Is he high on something? Pax asked what position Dog's operation had need of him.

The militia leader didn't answer. Instead he used his cigarette as a pointer, signaling to the main room.

"Most people ask about the sniper. The other Americans did." Dog's mouth hung open.

"For sure." The mannequin, Pax realized. That's what he wants to talk about. "Whatever you're willing to share."

"Disarmed the orc myself." Dog's voice turned wistful and coarse. "Found him on a rooftop. I came up from behind, he was deep in his scope, hunting for ukrop. Caught with no spotter. Goat-shit amateur. I choked him and beat his skull against the ledge and told him in his own language I would ass-rape his corpse if he defied me.

"Now I pack drones into supply trucks. I spend every day in meetings, screaming at government faggots. There is glory in Mariupol. And I am here, in the other Ukraine."

Dog set his cigarette down between his feet and began to cry.

Pax sat there, listening. He cleared his throat, which didn't shake Dog from his tears. He asked if he should leave.

The other man kept to his sobs. Fuck it, Pax thought. This is insane.

"Maybe their definition of National Idea is different than yours."

The militia leader stirred from his trance. He looked up, into Pax's face, the redness from his cheeks flushing down into the heavy veins in his neck. "Politics?"

"Aren't they related—war and politics? One's an extension of the other."

Dog made another scratching sound with his throat, then picked up the cigarette on the floor. He stood, cracked his neck, and walked into the main room. The smoke trailed him like a wraith. After a few seconds' consideration, Pax did, too.

"Those maps by the entrance," Dog said in front of him, "are of Kievan Rus', back when the Kremlin was a forest for bandits." He was about as tall as Pax, twice as wide, and moved through his personal museum with a slight hitch. "U-S-A! You all know nothing and do not apologize for it. I admire this. Reset minds. To remember is important, but to know how to forget? That is real power."

They stopped at the mannequin. Dog straightened its uniform collar.

"My little green man. A farm boy, from Dagestan. Pimples, bird neck. He had never traveled before, never even been to Moscow. After the battle, I went to his tent. I gave him coffee and a biscuit bar. He told me his name, his school, where he fucked his first girl. He told me he was sorry for being on that roof, said he'd never squeezed the trigger on his gun, not once. I asked what was the worst thing he had done in the war. He told me he took a steam iron from a house in Crimea. He said Ukrainians were Slavic brothers. He said he would return the iron and tell all Russian boys to never become soldiers for Putin.

"But. Brothers do not invade the land of brothers. Brothers do not steal from the land of brothers. I put my revolver between his teeth and told him to make his last confessions. He shitted himself, right there in the tent. A child far from home and much beyond himself, but also a soldier, an invader. I asked, 'You tell me the truth about never squeezing your trigger?' He nodded yes, promised on his mother's name.

"Then I said, 'That is too bad. Because I have.'"

Pax was watching the Ukrainian sidelong, the other man smoking, smirking to himself. He followed up, both because he knew he was expected to and because he wanted to know.

"Did you, then? Pull the trigger?"

"There's a video." The veins in Dog's neck were now throbbing. "A man I know, his friend from childhood, fought at the battle for the airport. They were encircled, captured.

"For sport, for propaganda, the vatniks tie this man's hands and legs to stakes on the ground. He is screaming, pleading, praying. Even he seems to not believe they will actually do this. They jeer as their sergeant pulls out a utility knife. They laugh louder when he talks about sausage and potatoes. He walks to the man, kicks open his legs, and slams the knife into the bottom of his balls." Dog mimicked the stabbing action against the mannequin. A thud echoed through the dim room, the mannequin rocking back and forth. "He carves them, like slices at the deli. He lifts them to the camera as a trophy and says in Russian, 'No more wheat children from here.' The others laugh more. Then they shoot the Ukrainian, like it's an act of mercy.

"Politics?" Dog stubbed out his cigarette against the mannequin and flicked it into a corner. "No. This is what the government faggots refuse to hear. Politics are for peace."

Pax knew now, if he hadn't all along, he didn't belong here. More importantly, he didn't want to be here. It's past time, he thought, to leave. Still. He was curious.

"What do you need? Those other guys, they have unique skills. They're connected to a whole world of industry and professionals. I'm just, well. I'm a motor inspector."

Dog strolled toward the tridents of gold, gripping one in his fists as if he intended to wrest it from its base. "I need

Westerners to . . . facil-tate? Transports east. Your passports help with stupid questions. Easy money for you."

"Oh." Pax smiled. He thought he'd have to lie to get off this floor, to get away from this man. "I gave mine away. It's hard to explain."

Dog let go of the trident and tilted his head, looking across the room at Pax like a third arm had emerged from his chest. "You—you gave away your passport?"

"I did."

Dog began laughing and returned to the smaller room. He reached it, still laughing, and slammed the door behind him. The laughter stayed with Pax all the way to the stairwell.

———

Pax figured he'd spend his afternoon riding the street tram. He knew he was overdue an exit strategy, he had access to the loft for only a few more days. But he couldn't leave without knowing what'd happened to Lee. If not for himself, at least for the family. He told himself he'd talk to Bogdan about it later and pulled out his headphones and MP3 player. What about Svitlana, and Taras and Kherson? That no longer concerned him, he thought, and probably never should have. She must already know. She must. Huddled in against the cold window, he thought about his encounter with an honest-to-Christ nationalist militia leader while listening to "In the Aeroplane Over the Sea." His mind ebbed and drifted through memory, and then through imagination.

A few minutes later, maybe an hour, perhaps longer, the intense chattering and aggravated gazes of surrounding passengers got Pax to remove his headphones and follow their focus. Dark plumes were scarring the cold sky to their east. Someone was making the sound of a loud jet engine with their lips and someone else speaking Ukrainian inserted an English phrase into their sentence, plopping it in like a thumb into a pie: "Cruise missiles."

At the next stop, Pax joined a group of young men running toward the rising swells of smoke.

He passed villas and apartment blocks, vaguely recognizing the neighborhood but not certain why. A crowd had formed around a crumbled building and he followed the young men pushing their way through it. He saw a body pinned under a beam and another being dragged out by its arms, bloody and moaning with a leg bone snapped out of its chute. He went to help a woman tossing away hunks of brick and stone, finding nothing underneath but a dark hollow cavity. The woman glided away and Pax began doing the same thing in another spot with someone else. At some point through the sweat and labor he understood they were sifting through the remnants of a church, there were so much dome cladding, so many shards of bright stained glass. His hands became cut and torn but he kept working, trying to keep up with the hysteria around him. Blood ran from his palms, wetting the rubble. A man with vacant eyes pulled a hymnal from the wreckage, shielded in its blue cover, not one page bent. The man began cackling to himself. Pax helped free a cat by holding up a long slab of metal cracked in its middle while another man reached down and pulled the animal from a snarl of debris. The cat didn't make a sound and had lost a long patch of fur along its side but otherwise looked as if it would be okay. It was only a cat, Pax thought, but it still felt like something. Later he helped carry a stretcher with a babusya on it. The old woman was under a blanket, making noises of gurgling anguish, and Pax resisted the urge to look under and see. There were more moans and the black smells of vomit and human waste and a torso in a crimson-sodden dress that everyone kept circling around to avoid, pretending it wasn't there.

Then, all at once, he was useless again. He found himself drinking from a warm bottled water someone had handed him and he looked around and realized the work was done, or what remained now belonged to the firefighters on scene. Blood and grime from his hands smeared the plastic bottle and he wiped them on his pants. To his flank, a pair of firefighters stepped away from a large object they'd finished dousing. Pax walked to it. It was a church bell, horizontal on its side and burnished black from the missile fire. Extinguisher smoke rose from it and contaminated the air. Pax looked again into the ruins, seeing sea-green cladding among the brick and stone. We were just here, he thought. A few evenings back. We stopped under the bell tower and listened to the chimes and I made the worst prayer ever.

He then noticed the boy across the street. He stood among a group of onlookers but also apart, alone. He wore an overlong soccer hoodie and kept sweeping at his black bangs and as Pax walked to him, calling Denys's name, he saw that the boy was watching the aftermath of the strike from the sides of his eyes.

The chocolate house lay diagonally to them. It looked just fine to Pax, untouched, like most of the surrounding area, giving the day a sudden dissonance.

"Hey," he said.

Denys did not respond.

"Hey," he tried again. The boy did not respond again. "Let's get you home."

Denys did not move, continuing to stare past Pax with the sides of his eyes. He began walking once Pax nudged him. He didn't say much of anything as they walked alongside one another. When the boy did speak, it was in a low, faraway hush, in impenetrable Ukrainian. The only word Pax could understand was "tato."

Dad.

Denys prided himself on being a good son. So when his mother told him to go to bed, he'd obliged. She couldn't make him sleep, though. Only his dad's stories about pirates and elves held that power. No one else told them the same. No one else told them right.

His mom wasn't like other parents. She didn't volunteer at his school, didn't chat up his teacher, didn't let him go to sleepovers, even when he got invited to one. She was omnipresent, alone at drop-off, alone at pickup, but always there, always on time. His father worked often and worked late, so it was usually just the two of them, going to playgrounds and parks, exploring different parts of the city. On the rare occasions Denys got annoyed by his mother's—what had Nazar's father called it, hovering?—he willed it away.

It was fine. It was okay. Deep within himself, in a place he didn't have words for, Denys understood his mom needed him as much as he needed her.

So when the American took him home that afternoon,

delivering him like a present, he'd felt only shame and humiliation. Her face was flushed and tear-streaked and she'd squeezed him in a hug until he demanded she stop. "Where were you?" she kept asking. "Where were you?" and no matter how many times he answered, she didn't seem to hear him.

The American had stayed for dinner. Then came Denys's bedtime. His mom had checked on him, then returned downstairs, talking with the stranger for hours. He'd heard them both use his name, and his dad's, over and over, and then something about one of the cities in the south. The rest he couldn't translate. They were speaking too quickly. His English was not as good as Nazar's.

Denys thought again about the man they'd pulled from the rubble of the church. He'd never seen a dead body before. It'd been carried right past him. No different than a fish at the market, he thought, just guts and slop and bone. He wondered if that's what he looked like inside, too. He didn't think God would allow him to look like that but he didn't know. He'd never really thought about it before.

He didn't like that the American was still in the house. The man smelled of fruity deodorant but moved like a scared bird. Denys didn't like the way he talked slow at him and didn't like the way he looked at his mom. He hadn't heard the front door open or close. He'd know if it had. His eyes weren't good but he could hear better than anyone. Nazar called it a superpower, sometimes, when he was being nice.

He looked across his bedroom at his race-car clock. The digits were fuzzy. He walked to it. It was a few minutes shy of midnight. Late enough, he thought. She won't get mad.

He opened his door and listened. Nothing went but the hum of the dishwasher. He moved down the stairs and through the home like a little mouse. He enjoyed these late-night patrols, they provided a spooky physical thrill. And he imagined during them. Sometimes he was a brave voyager looking for an ancient temple in the jungle. Other times he was an astronaut who'd crash-landed on an unknown planet. Still other times, he became his dad, stalking Russians in the distant east.

Elvis lay draped across the floor of the kitchen, the animal's eyes refracting with recognition of one of its humans. Denys moved into the living room. His ears hunted the shadows and found nothing while his eyes settled over a hazy mound on the couch. A faint voice startled him. He jumped back into the entryway of the kitchen.

"Hey there."

It was the stranger. The man lay under a blanket with his socked feet propped over the couch arm. Denys was embarrassed he'd been surprised in his own house. He knew he'd shown it, too. He listened to the race of his heart and stepped back into the room.

"Hello," he said. When the stranger didn't say anything he continued. "I'm going to my mom's room."

"Makes sense."

"Why are you here?"

"No trams this late." The man's voice sounded strained, confused. Denys decided he didn't want to be around it. He passed adjacent to the couch.

"You okay?" the stranger asked. Denys stopped and looked toward the shape of the man's face. "Today was some heavy stuff."

Heavy. Stuff. Denys turned over the English words in his mouth and mind. He figured the man meant the dead body.

"Yes," he said. "Are you okay?"

The man didn't answer. Denys waited a few seconds, then continued past the couch into his mom's room and crawled into bed with her.

VIII

Voices at the door tore Pax from a dream. He'd had a lurid one earlier and tried to return to it but its successor involved a church bell and a judgmental woman with a drooping eye. "Why are you here?" she kept asking, and when he pointed to the bell between them, she'd kept shaking her head. He sat up on the couch and rubbed at a dull crick in his neck, the taste of stale citrus in his mouth. He was too groggy to even try to decipher what was happening at the door. His hands twinged from the aches and cuts and he flexed them both out. Then he reached for his boots.

The wave of cruise missiles had ended sometime the evening before, though the sirens never had. They'd struck a local tank plant and a fuel depot and an empty hillside that sprouted into a brush fire. And the church, of course, no one anywhere could stop talking about the church, and while Pax didn't want to admit it and would never say it out loud, he knew how sometimes things happened in war, coordinates got messed up, wires got crossed, the pogue pressing the button sneezed. One time in Afghanistan a mosque in their valley had been turned to cinder by a gunship in the sky, and it'd been an accident, a mistake, he refused to believe American pilots would ever purposefully do it. Maybe the Russians are different, he thought. He didn't know. Maybe they intended collateral damage, maybe their officers allowed for more of it. Or they'd just fucked up. He doubted it mattered to the dead.

You brought the boy here, Pax thought. You brought him home. It was a good thing to do.

Daylight leaked through the room's shuttered windows, telling him it was midmorning. His phone confirmed it. Cognizance came in bits: the boy standing in the entryway of the kitchen, still in his pajamas and petting the cat. Pax followed his lead and homed in on the conversation at the door. Svitlana was speaking with curtness, not unusual for her except there was a simmer to it, a naked heat that belied her clipped words. The other voice belonged to Yeva, calm but exaggerated in its evenness, the way people talked when they believed tone could serve as a verbal guardrail. Yeva clicked her tongue. Svitlana inhaled sharply and exhaled slowly, as if to steady herself. Pax looked back to the boy. Denys had his head cocked so he could focus his ears and vision, together.

The two women entered the house. Pax sat up on the couch, pushing his feet into the soles of his boots. Behind him, he heard the boy step forward.

Svitlana said something to her son. He said something back. She nodded and issued something that sounded very much like an order. He said something else back. Yeva forced a hard smile. No one in the room said anything to Pax, nor did they look his way. It was like he wasn't even there at all.

Pax watched the boy shamble out and walk up to his room. He waited for the creaking of stairs to stop before turning to the women. Both were staring into the empty space of corners, far gone to the place of invisible ills and impossible ends.

"What's going on?" he asked. Yeva shot him a ferocious glare so he added, "Sorry," but Svitlana's eyes found him with something more like pity. Not unlike, he thought, the way she'd just been looking at her son.

"It's Taras," she said. "They have him, and now I must go get him."

He was alive, at least. Yeva didn't have all the details but she had learned that a squad of Ukrainian marines had managed to get the man to a frontline clinic in a village north of Mykolaiv. Then they'd returned to the zero line, back to their country's existential fight for survival. The southern front was a mess, a hotbed of scattered units and amorphous, shifting positions. The Russians seemed hell-bent on Odesa. Every gun between them and there mattered.

Taras, meanwhile, was mired in his own existential fight. Bullet wounds or shrapnel—the people who talked to the people who talked to Yeva had mentioned both—had collapsed one of his lungs. The clinic had been able to insert a chest tube but that was a temporary measure. He needed surgery, and soon. Which meant evacuating to a hospital in the rear.

By the time they arrived at Yeva's, Pax thought he had mostly pieced together what was now happening. The Ukrainian military couldn't spare a medevac for one misplaced reservist, everything in the south was too chaotic. A group of foreign civilians had accepted the task, then balked—it was too close to the Russian advance, they said. So Nove Zavtra was handling it. And Svitlana was insisting she go with them, for reasons either lost in translation or never uttered to begin with.

There was a despair to the movement, an unspoken gloom that was allayed only if someone was putting on false cheer for Denys. Pax figured she was going to identify the body and escort it home. In front of Yeva's gate, they found Bogdan and Unknown loading a black, full-size cargo van with jugs of water and cans of fuel. A long, narrow space was kept clear in the back. Pax saw it was big enough for either a stretcher or a body bag.

The Ukrainian recruiter began shouting at Svitlana in their language as soon as he saw them. She yelled right back. Bogdan pointed at the boy, which infuriated her even more. Pax pulled a stuffed dragon from Denys's sleepover pack.

"Who's this?" Pax asked.

"That's Chudo," the boy said.

"Afghans tell legends about a dragon they say once lived in their mountains. It's crazy how so many different cultures have similar stories."

"Okay," the boy said.

Pax suggested he go set down his things in the house. Denys agreed. The boy began walking up the driveway. Yeva attempted to intervene in the argument while Unknown kept to his loading duty. Pax felt removed from it all, a spectator to a drama that at once fascinated and excluded him. Should Svitlana go east? He didn't know. His homeland had never been invaded. He'd never had an almost ex-husband. She was brave, he knew that. As the boy disappeared up the driveway, the youngest Boyko, Roman, ambled down it, wearing a hoodie, gym shorts, and foam clogs. He looked hungover to Pax, his face bright pink and puffy. After taking in the shouting, he sought out explanation.

Pax told what he could. The younger man cleaned his glasses with a sleeve as he listened, making a neutral grunt when he learned about Taras's condition.

"This must be awkward for you," he said. "I will be real, it is odd that you are still here."

Pax thought about that. "Yeah," he said.

"Maverick, you did an incredibly brave thing." He was quoting *Top Gun* again. "But your ego is writing checks your body can't cash."

Pax ignored him. You brought the boy home, he thought again. It's your turn.

Bogdan now seemed to be pleading with Svitlana. Her arms were crossed and her jaw set, her linebacker shoulders squared and full. She was absorbing the man's edicts with the mask of the rational, like she actually was hearing him and considering what he had to say, as if she hadn't anticipated this very song and dance. She'd get her way, Pax knew. She was adamant like that.

"He's embarrassed," Roman observed. "It's bad enough he feels himself a toy soldier while the big war happens. Then his army cannot help Chernenko, one of their own. Now a woman refuses to listen to his order to stay." He loosed a low whistle and put back on his glasses.

They watched Svitlana shake her head yet again.

"Fine." Bogdan's sudden English broke the lullaby of passive observation. He gestured at Pax. "He comes, too. It is a long trip."

Pax comprehended what was being asked of him through the muddle of a beautiful day. East. Toward the war. Next to the war, adjacent to it. Not into it, though. Through checkpoints and logistical hubs and maybe some artillery positions. But that's it, he thought, you can do that. Bogdan was staring at him. He looked back. He thought about Lee, and their visit together to the old town when they'd first met this justice who sat in the back of a café upon his metal legs. Svitlana was saying something dismissive but he didn't hear her, he could do only so many things in a moment. Not into the war, he thought again. It's a clinic. He held himself to the recruiter's icy gaze.

"So now I get selected," he said.

"You should've told me you are a mechanic," Bogdan said. "We have maintenance units."

Pax took a slow yoga breath and rubbed at the prayer beads wrapped around his wrist. His hands hurt so much from the rescue work at the church. Then he managed a half grin, which itself gave him the courage to keep going. "Sure," he said. "Let's ride."

Svitlana spun around and began yelling at him, first in rushed Ukrainian, then in English. "No," she said, "no. We don't need you. This is something I must do for my family. You need to go home, Luke."

"I want to help."

"We don't need you."

"You might. I fix things."

"This isn't your life." She was flustered, angry at him in a way he hadn't seen for many years. Probably not since Milan, he thought. Not since then. "Don't you dare do that thing that makes everything in the world about you. I will not let it happen."

Pax put his hands on her shoulders. He saw fury on her face, torment, as well, and for once, maybe the first time, he understood how little of it had to do with him.

"Listen, please," he said, something he repeated until he saw that she was. "If nothing else, I'm another pair of hands to carry the stretcher. Then you'll never see me again, if that's what you want. I promise. But I can help. Let me."

He let his arms go slack and to his side. He heard no sound anymore blaring from his chest. He felt sun on his lips and skin. Spring was nearing. Her eyes fell away to the ground.

They finished loading the van in strained silence. Denys came back down the driveway to hug his mother. So too did Roman, returning with a canvas messenger bag and wearing an embroidered, collared shirt with blue-on-white stitching. Little sundials were sewn into its pattern. It was the same type of shirt, Pax noticed, that his father and brother had worn the night of the dinner party.

"Commander," Roman said to Bogdan, who was looking at him with only the slightest hint of surprise. "Let us go do what the army is too chickenshit for."

Yeva stood at the gate with her arms around Denys as the group piled into the van. Unknown claimed the driver's seat. Bogdan took the command position as the front passenger. Roman clambered into the back, leaving the middle row for Svitlana and Pax.

The boy blew a kiss at his mom, which she returned. She rolled down her window and said something in Ukrainian. A lone quiver entered her voice but she swallowed it away and said it again, straight. The boy nodded, blank-faced.

IX

They departed Lviv at half past noon, escaping a snarl of traffic in the eastern suburbs thirty minutes later. Google said the journey would take twelve hours. Bogdan said they'd make it in ten. Roman raised his hand from the back.

"Urinate in an empty bottle if you need to," Bogdan said. Roman lowered his hand.

Territorial defense ran the checkpoint that led to the highway. Bogdan flashed some sort of credential and they were waved past the inspection line. Unknown shifted the van into sixth gear and they began barreling through the bright of afternoon. Pax's seat belt was lodged under the row; he kept yanking but it wouldn't free. Bogdan turned the radio to a Ukrainian news station and put a large wad of dip into his mouth. Svitlana stared out her window with her body shifted aslant, about as far from anyone as she could get. From his messenger bag, Roman pulled out a box of powdered donuts. Pax took two and passed forward the box.

His right leg was twitching. He watched it go with docile interest, as if it belonged to another being, another body. He heard Lee's voice in his head with yet another maxim: "Being brave doesn't mean you ain't scared. Being brave means being scared and doing it anyhow."

A bit childish, Pax thought. But also true. A few minutes later his leg stopped. He pulled out his phone and scrolled for war updates.

An hour passed, then another. Most vehicles pushed the other way, back west, but not all. Pax looked out his window as urban sprawl relented to farmscape. The land was flat and rambling, agrarian in a way that if he squinted, he could pretend it was rural Nebraska or Iowa. Wheat fields rose galore, months from harvest, pale-green and light-yellow stalks straining up to the sky in a blend. Through towns and villages he saw onion domes and steeples and gas stations and stoplights, and then the land was back, flat as ever, rambling as ever, a gentle wind rolling through the crop.

"It's like a postcard," he said. His voice broke the still in the van that'd held since leaving Lviv. "No wonder everyone wants it."

"The blue of the sky. The yellow of the field." Bogdan spoke through his wad of dip with something approaching awe. "When we first met, Corporal Paxton, I told you that Ukraine means 'the borderlands' in old Slavic. Which is true. But it is only one translation. Others called it 'the wilderness' or 'the wild fields.' Especially where we go now, in the south and east." He trickled a gob of dip from his mouth into an empty plastic bottle. "This is what we must force them to understand. It was never theirs to miss."

Unknown nodded in agreement. He switched lanes and sped their van by a plodding medical Humvee. A half minute passed. Pax could almost feel Roman in the back unable to contain himself.

"Our warrior-poet speaks lovely truths," Roman said. "Until victory!"

"Silence, clown," Bogdan replied. Then he turned up the radio.

"He's not wrong. It's even better in early summer." Roman again held out the box of donuts to Pax. "If we ever take back Crimea, that's where I will be. Making peace with Russian women in the clubs of Yalta."

Pax looked across his row at Svitlana's still-twisted body.

She was breathing like she was asleep but in the reflection of the glass he saw her open eyes, watching the passing scenery. He wanted to know how she was feeling, what she was thinking, but she wanted to be left alone, so he'd do that. She's probably hungry, he thought. He poked her with the box of donuts. She shook her head.

A few minutes later Pax's phone rang. It was Merriman. He didn't like the idea of disturbing the equilibrium everyone had settled into, but it'd been two days since Yavoriv. He couldn't let it ring out.

"Yo, Paxton." If the other man still stewed over what had been said in the coffeehouse he made no mention of it. "Still no sign of Lee. They've been sorting through and identifying folks, too, so not sure what to make of that. Ukrainian mil did give clearance to send someone there to claim his personal effects—might give you the opportunity to look around, find someone who actually knows what's what. Wanna go?"

"I'm headed east now." The world was funny, sometimes, Pax thought, how so often obligations went one way and desires the other. "Helping evac a wounded reservist. I could get up there tomorrow, maybe? Or the day after. Definitely then."

There was a long silence on the other end of the line.

"How far east?"

"Little north of Mykolaiv. Some village with a clinic. Driving there now."

"Oh boy." An artificial chuckle came through the speaker, and Pax couldn't help but resent it. "Highly recommend you take a tactical pause. Things down there are—fluid. There's no telling where the lines will be ten minutes from now, let alone a few hours."

"Can't," Pax said. No one else in the van was looking at him but he could feel their attention. "It's very urgent. Need to get him out ASAP."

"Paxton, I may have already lost one of you—" The other man stopped himself and sighed. "Keep me apprised, okay? Send me the grid coordinates, at least. I'll try to keep you updated with the advance . . . I know some people." Merriman then chuckled again, but this one seemed normal, even genuine. "You always marched to the beat of your own drum, man. Who is this guy? Better be someone special for this cowboy shit."

"I guess." From the corner of his eye, he looked at Svitlana's reflection in the glass of the side window and watched her watch him. "A friend of a friend."

Just beyond the river near Vinnytsia, angling more and more south, Svitlana turned from the window and spoke. The openness of the day had given way to a leaden dusk and the sun was sinking against their backs. A collection of brake lights and merging lanes suggested another checkpoint lay in wait.

"Thank you," she said. "All of you. This means more than you know. That people like you still exist in this world, well." Her eyes moved from person to person in the van. Pax looked away first so she didn't have to. "Thank you," she said again.

"When we get south." Authority filled Bogdan's voice. "We will drop Svita and Roman at a military safe house before going into the village." The younger man objected but gained no position. This compromise had already been brokered in Lviv. "She has a boy to consider. And you must see her back if we do not return."

The checkpoints coming out of the west had all been manned by territorial defense. Different oblasts had different techniques but they'd all been mostly staffed by everyday middle-aged people pressed into duty. As their van crept forward, this checkpoint began revealing itself as more intricate. The soldiers here had edges instead of flab, moved with pointed familiarity, and were kitted out with flak vests and scopes on their rifles. Bogdan held up his credential to an armed guard, who only shook his head. Pax listened to hostile Ukrainian going out of the van, then coming into it. A second guard approached, then a bearded supervisor type. Bogdan looked at Unknown, grimaced with his brow, then got out of the van.

Pax followed. He knew what this was. He'd seen them in Afghanistan.

Beyond the checkpoint, a flock of birds was perched on a power line strung between utility poles, seeming to watch the exchange as from a gallery. Bogdan had taken the guards to the back of the van and was holding up a can of fuel. "We might need that," Pax said. He pulled out Lee's roll of money and held it out.

"You all accept dollars?"

They did. He handed over most of what remained, keeping a lucky bill for himself. Appreciate it, big fella, Pax thought. It felt like Lee, wherever he was, was still looking out for him.

The two men returned to their seats. Their van was waved through.

Everyone sat in quiet for a minute. Then Roman said something in Ukrainian, which made even Bogdan smile. "What was all that?" Pax asked.

"Nationalists from this oblast." Bogdan sniffed contemptuously and reached for more dip. "They heard my Galician accent and charged double. Small-time bullshit but any war brings out the—" He paused and plucked at his beard while he searched for a word. "Grubbers."

"A wise man once told me," Pax said, "to always check their shoes and watches. That's how you know where they're at on the totem pole." No one here will get that analogy, he thought. So then he told the van about his meeting the day before with Dog, what the militia leader had wanted from him, and how the man burst into a crying fit over his fighters becoming famous for battling in the steel plant while he wasn't there.

"Can't even begin to describe the sounds he was making," Pax said, "with those damn ribs."

"He—he is mafia." Roman began laughing from the back, a raw, guttural release that pealed through the vehicle. "You had lunch with one of Lviv's most dangerous criminals. He showed you his museum. And then you told him he couldn't even use you for your passport?"

"Not even lunch!" Bogdan was laughing just as hard from the front seat, trying to speak through gasps. "He had to watch the man eat while he sat there and waited!"

Svitlana laughed now, too. Even Unknown looked amused. Pax leaned into his role.

"Dumb American move, I guess," to which Svitlana said,

"No," as Roman said, "Yes!" which sent the van into another fit of hysterics.

They kept south on the highway, and east, striking into the young evening against the wind.

They were a few hours out when the rain began. The headlights of bus convoys hurried west, over and over, a chain of fleeing beams. Theirs was the only civilian vehicle going the other way. At checkpoint after checkpoint, Bogdan showed his credential and argued their purpose.

Svitlana pointed out the road signs. Some had been scorched, others marked over. Still others had been removed from their posts and absconded with. Unknown said something low to the steering wheel.

"Make them use their Soviet maps," Bogdan translated, which Pax thought was cool, but also ominous.

Roman suggested they come up with some code words. Pax saw Bogdan roll his eyes through the rearview mirror.

"I read of it online," Roman continued. "People in the occupied territories do this. To make sure people are who they say they are."

"A small comfort," Svitlana said. "Why not?"

"Veselka." Bogdan turned and peered at the rest of them,

his arcane scrutiny racing through the depths of the van. He repeated the word again, then translated. "Rainbow. The orcs have difficulty with the soft *e*."

Pax looked out again at the wet night, rain streaks smearing across the window like finger paint. All he could see was an empty, dark field with a murky tree line beyond it. Who the hell, he thought, would be talking about rainbows tonight?

Sometime later the van began to overheat. Unknown pulled over to the shoulder of the highway.

"Anyone know how long Nove Zavtra's had this?" Pax asked.

"My sister acquired it, maybe, two days back," Roman said. "Used piece of shit."

"Right" was all Pax said. He saw strain and worry on Svitlana's face. They were nowhere close to anywhere and as far from anywhere as her dying husband.

They waited until he felt certain the engine had cooled. Then Pax got out. Flashlight between his teeth, the rain lashed over his vision and clothes, the water like tonic in the cuts of his hands. He opened the hood and rubbed along the radiator hoses, hoping for a leak there. On the radiator itself he found a hairline crack in the near tank. Coolant seeped out in a little trail. It wasn't big yet and he thought it could be managed but he wasn't sure. He grabbed a quarter-full jug of coolant from the back and poured in its contents. Bogdan came out with the repair kit. There was no real epoxy in it, only some sort of synthetic casting glue.

"This is gonna be patchwork as fuck," he said. "Here, shield the radiator and hold the light."

He did what he could. He filed out the length of the crack to create a groove. He kept drying the repair with his sleeves and then the bottom of his undershirt. They didn't have any fill powder so he ran some glue into the groove, then pushed in the fiberglass mesh. He ran another line of glue over that and folded the mesh in on itself. Then he took a lighter to the work, trying to melt and congeal it.

Unknown started the engine again, then revved it. The temperature gauge said they were good but Pax saw tendrils of steam rising through the rain. He wished he was in a proper garage and not in the messy night. He wished they weren't facing such a time crunch.

"Probably only slowed the leak," he said, getting back into the van. "Couple hours if we're lucky."

Bogdan handed him a dry fleece sweatshirt and looked at Svitlana.

"Aren't you glad I suggested he come?"

The tension in her face had eased but not vanished. The

van pulled back on the highway, Unknown gunning it faster than Pax would've recommended. "I am," she said. She leaned over and squeezed his elbow.

It grew darker. Fewer village lights scattered the horizon. Streetlamps turned meager. Roman said it felt like they were in space. Later he said his cell phone had lost reception. Everyone else pulled out theirs as if on command. It was true, Pax saw, his phone gathering zero bars. He had an unread text, sent fifty minutes before: Merriman telling him they needed to steer clear of Mykolaiv itself, but the villages north should be okay.

"Keep me apprised," the text demanded. Pax powered off his phone to save some of its battery.

―――――――

Bogdan opened his window and Pax could smell sea in the air. He liked how it washed through his nostrils and mouth so he took another breath of it, deep and long.

"We are nearing the safe house," Bogdan said. Roman had been sleeping in the back. He shouted until the younger man sat up and kept his eyes open.

A large, dimmed spotlight guided them into an immense checkpoint with razor wire layered across the width of the highway. Pax saw that it was manned not by territorial defense or militia but with real Ukrainian soldiers who wore patches of the shield and trident. One began directing them back the other way with a flashlight. Unknown stopped the vehicle, the engine still running. Bogdan got out into the rain, holding out his credential.

The first soldier seemed confused, as did the second. Through the rain they watched Bogdan gesticulating with his hands, his frustration coming to the van muffled but plain. "It is not going right," Roman said. The recruiter was pointed to a long concrete building Pax figured was a rest-area bathroom in normal times. Under the building's overhang, a man in a camouflage raincoat shook his head at Bogdan once, then again, and again. Then another man in a camouflage raincoat approached. He hugged Bogdan with enthusiasm, and Bogdan reciprocated in kind.

"Hugs," Roman said. "Hugs are good."

A few minutes later, Bogdan got back in the van, his English almost popping off his tongue. "The gods favor us," he said. "I fought alongside that major at Ilovaisk."

"Seems like a great guy."

"Total asshole. He made his men clean his weapon for him." Bogdan cracked his neck. "He will get us through but no civilians can stay in the safe house. There is a general here. He and his staff have filled it."

Everyone let that drift through the van, lingering with what it meant, what it didn't.

"This is good," Svitlana finally said. "I want to go forward."

"Yes," Roman said.

Pax felt torn but Svitlana was looking at him for support. "For what it's worth," he said, holding out his phone, "my old captain says the villages north of the city are clear. He's CIA or something. He'd know."

Bogdan's eyes narrowed but a sound of acquiescence came out of him. "Yes," he said. "That is what they have told me, as well."

Unknown shifted into first gear and the van began moving. Svitlana leaned over again to squeeze Pax's elbow. "Thank you," she mouthed.

He shrugged and pretended like everything was fine.

They edged through the remainder of the checkpoint, then followed a long line of orange cones to a highway exit that directed them to an old truss bridge. The van's wheels rumbled up and onto the beams. The bridge spanned a thin ribbon of low water. The spotlight from the highway illuminated a stretch farther up the river canal. Pax looked there and saw another short bridge that had been blown apart. Its ends clung to the banks but the middle had fallen into the canal and black water ran over it as rain fell upon it. They rolled off the beams and onto a paved, two-lane road.

Pax heard sharp, flaring breathing from behind him. He turned to show he would listen.

"What is the English word for the storm in the ocean? A big one." Roman's face was pale, maybe even nauseated. How scared did I look, Pax wondered, our first day in Wardak?

"Hurricane."

"It looks like a hurricane hit there." He meant the bridge, or the void where the bridge had been.

"No." Svitlana's voice was adamantine. "That was man-made."

No one said anything. Pax made brief eye contact with Bogdan through the rearview mirror as the other man reached again for his dip. The rain persisted, the wiper blades slushing against the windshield.

———————

A black-and-white sign with a long, Slavic name marked entry to the village. They moved through a roundabout. A fountain sat in the center island, across which the blue-and-yellow bicolor stretched languid. Everything was dark and still and Bogdan told Unknown to kill the van's headlights. They drove by a church, a post office, then a dormant shadow of a barn. To their flank, a bright green flare shot into the sky, and Pax saw Bogdan's neck crane in interest. They passed another church. Pax sniffed again at the half-open window. It wasn't sea dampness he found in the air anymore, but something else. He considered what.

It was the smell of distant burning.

Bogdan directed the van left through another roundabout. They crunched through a deep pothole brimming with rainwater. The wiper blades sang against the windshield. There were remote claps of fireworks that Pax knew were anything but, then a counter patter that sounded somewhat closer. His body became taut and his mind a probe, something hyper and primal juicing his veins. Bogdan opened the glove compartment and pulled a pistol from it and handed it back to him. A round was already chambered and the safety on and he tucked the gun into a fleece pocket. Roman and Svitlana were asking questions in Ukrainian, not loud but insistent, while Bogdan pointed to an approaching dirt path. They kept chattering and he kept ignoring, and they kept chattering and he kept ignoring. Unknown made the turn.

Down the path an outline of a squat building began to emerge. It was one story and low-roofed and Bogdan told them they were here.

He had them stay in the van while he verified. He dashed

into the wet night. A few seconds later a porch light was roused. Rain hitting the roof echoed through the van as if they were in a cave. Everyone could hear everyone else fidgeting, breathing. Pax fondled the pistol in his pocket, brushing a thumb against his phone. He pulled that out and powered it back on. A string of six unread texts awaited, all from Merriman.

> "Bad guys pushing north of Myko now too. Stop where you're at, hang tight"
>
> "It's a mess down there, man. Turn around. DO NOT CROSS THE RIVER"
>
> "The main battle's for the city itself but they still have scout units operating northward"
>
> "Yo! You getting these???"
>
> "Paxton, get back to me as soon as you read this"
>
> "It's impossible to get a good read on anything around Myko . . . hunker down!!"

He'd also tried to call twice.

Well, Pax thought. This explains the star cluster.

He could feel his thoughts jumping and his senses buckling but then Bogdan was back at the van, shouting at them to follow through the rain. So he did, hearing the slap of his boots in mud and feeling the sting of hard rain against his neck and cheeks. Then he and the group were under a porch, being ushered into a dry, airless space.

It was a waiting room. A framed wooden portrait of the Virgin Mary hung along the back wall alongside a painted red cross. Candles blazed through the room as electric light spilled in from an adjoining hallway; a steady generator hum from that direction explained the discrepancy. Bogdan shoved hand towels at them. At the nub of the hallway a long bird of a woman stood in scrubs with her arms crossed. Waiting, Pax saw, but for what?

Bogdan said something in Ukrainian. Svitlana dropped the hand towel she'd been drying her hair with and strode into the hallway with the nurse. Pax went to follow but Bogdan put a hand on his chest. "Family only," he said.

"Of course." There was an itch in Pax's throat he couldn't swallow away. "We too late?"

"Not at all." Bogdan's eyes sunk into him, seeking, perhaps, a reaction. "They say he's stabilized. He will live as long as he's operated on in the next day or so." Pax blinked and blinked, holding to the quiet. "Something like a miracle, they say."

"That's great." He said it because he knew he needed to, and because he meant it. "Much better to find a man than a body."

He told Bogdan about the texts. The other man was as

inscrutable as ever. He contemplated his reply to Merriman. His phone had 10 percent battery.

"All okay here," he typed. "Going offline. Will check back in when I can." Then he added a thumbs-up emoji and pressed send and powered off the phone.

Roman had seized a plastic chair in a corner under the holy mother. He looked wet and tired, affixed with a glazed-over stare. Pax took the seat next to him.

"You've lost that loving feeling," he said. "Talk to me, Goose."

Roman didn't respond and remained slumped in his chair. Pax left it alone. Sometimes, he thought, there's just nothing to be done.

Pax watched candlelight dance along the wall for a few minutes, the face of the portrait and the red paint of the cross gleaming in the flickers. He began thinking about what he'd do when they got back to Lviv. On to the base at Yavoriv, he figured, once he finished that, he'd be able to write Lee's ex-wife. Hell, he thought. Came out east and found a dead man alive. Could well happen again. Lee would laugh and call him a fucking jabroni when he explained how they thought the cruise missiles had gotten him, how they couldn't get ahold of him for a few days, and how he'd laid into Merriman at the coffeehouse because of it. And now he'd have a war story to share, too, war-adjacent, at least, something to assuage the humiliation of being rejected by the legion.

That thought more than anything drove him back outside, where the rain had lessened.

He smelled coolant as soon as he neared the van. He popped the hood and waited for the engine to finish cooling. He felt sure the radiator seal had broken but when he ran his fingers on the spot, he was surprised to find it'd held. Yet a puddle of coolant was collecting under the vehicle. He moved out the battery to discover the water pump was now leaking. The impeller had dislodged from the main shaft.

Must've been the pothole, Pax thought. They'd hit it so fast and too straight on. He heard the slap of boots in the mud approaching. It was Bogdan. He pressed a rag against the water pump. It sopped up coolant. When he let go it kept dripping more.

"The hospital in Odesa is two hours away. Can we get there?"

"Tough to say." Pax wanted to say yes but this wasn't a matter of mitigating a hairline crack. "Even if we went twenty miles an hour the whole way, the engine's still gonna be burning up. And the cylinder heads will warp, regardless."

"So?"

"So we need to go ask that nurse where she keeps her spare parts."

No one in the clinic knew anything about cars. The bird woman suggested a nearby junkyard. "Two thousand meters," she said. "Very close. I can draw a map."

Pax thought about it. Two thousand meters. A little over a mile. All eyes were on him. They could chance it, he knew—two hours to Odesa was possible. But what if the engine fried on the way, in the middle of nowhere? Then he'd be responsible for their failure, and Taras's life. Or death, his bleeding out in the empty rainy black on a forsaken stretch of highway far from the safety of Lviv. He pictured the olives in Svitlana's eyes quivering at him all over again, this time with rage, for failing her, after she'd come all this way to bring home her son's father. No, he'd fixed the van once and he'd do it again. Besides, the nurse told them it'd be another forty minutes until Taras was ready to transport. Why wait here when they could go there and look?

Bogdan agreed in his crisp manner. "I'll come, too," he said. "You remain to keep watch."

He'd been speaking to Unknown but it was Roman, still slumped in the chair against the wall, who replied.

"No problem, Commander. I am armed."

"You're what?"

Roman reached into his messenger bag and pulled out a pump-action shotgun, holding it from its barrel, flagging most everyone in the process. Bogdan yanked the weapon free and then cleared it in the corner. It was old, Pax saw, charcoal black and large-bored but shorter than Western-made shotguns. Once Bogdan stopped cursing, he asked what it was.

"KS-23. Soviet weapon for prison riots."

"You brought a gun, Roman?"

"This is a war, isn't it?"

"Where did you get a gun?"

"Where one keeps a gun. My dad's safe."

Bogdan instructed in Ukrainian; precise guidance for the weapon's use, complete with a sector of fire focused into the courtyard.

"Yes, Commander." He'd shed his malaise from earlier. Roman stood from his chair and saluted like a palace guard. "I will protect them with my life."

He was acting as if he was kidding but his face held real resolve. Bogdan and Pax headed out.

The rain had eased to a drizzle. The gloomy air and dark well of sky were mirrors of one another. A breeze swirled and cut through the courtyard. Something had been digging at Pax like a splinter.

"I guess I should thank you," he said.

"For?"

"If you hadn't rejected me, I'd have been at Yavoriv."

Pax listened to the other man load his own pistol, the black magic of the gun slamming forward.

"Perhaps." He clicked on a small red-lens flashlight. It gave them both a sort of fever vision. "Have you heard from your friend there?"

"No."

"Heroyam slava." He aimed the red light at Pax's fleece pocket. "You prepared to use that?"

"Wouldn't have taken it otherwise."

They moved into the village along the edge of a dirty, wet road. Pax refused to think about the gravity of what was happening so he didn't. They heard firing ahead of them. Bogdan made a hand-and-arm signal with his fist that Pax didn't understand, and the Ukrainian didn't clarify. An animal called through the still, searching and sharp. Nothing answered it. They passed a large farmhouse located up and off the road. It had been hit with an artillery shell. Even through the dark Pax could see its guts, sofas and bed frames twisted sideways and spilling out the opened face of the building. Another animal with round, translucent eyes watched them from a tree. They heard more firing. Bogdan's pace was diligent and held some bound to it; metal legs didn't seem all bad, Pax thought, only a stiff hitch at the top of a stride gave them away. A cottage appeared, nestled along a bend of the roadside. Faint candlelight trickled from its front window. Bogdan approached and peered in. He slunk past it and waved Pax forward. Through the window Pax glanced a table of people quietly playing a board game. They kept moving. How are we not there yet? he asked himself, seeing only Bogdan's little red dot. One mile, a measly mile, we've walked that three times over. They reached a little brook of smelly trash water and bore right, hugging the bank, now perpendicular to the sound of the guns. He realized he was stroking his prayer beads so he put his hand back in the pocket where it could instead stroke the pistol. Another post-storm gust stirred, sending traces of dirty water into his nostrils. He tried, failed, not to gag. From the direction of the road came the loud, mechanical groans of an armored vehicle. They paused, turned, and looked toward the noise. Then they kept going. About a hundred feet farther along the brook they stopped at a chain-link fence. Bogdan lifted up a flap from the bottom. Pax hunched and stepped through, into the junkyard.

His boots trampled gravel. It took a few seconds for his eyes to adjust but soon the silhouettes of vehicle hulls speckled his vision. He knew what he sought, and moved through the yard like a forager in the woods. Three sedans in a neat row weren't worth even looking into. A minibus shaped like a parallelogram gave him a burst of hope but the engine was a husk with nothing in it. He tried a truck that had a water pump too small, and an old station wagon with one too wide. He came across a bona fide Yugo hatchback from the eighties, and any other time in any other place he would've spent hours with it, tinkering around with the worst car ever designed. But he couldn't and kept moving through the yard, Bogdan a red-lens shadow at his heels.

They came to a grouping of large metal frames that stacked vehicles on three levels. More fire came from the same direction as before, though this was of the rapid machine-gun variety. Pax focused, as much as he could, on the cars. He saw a totaled minivan tucked in the corner that might have the water pump and a panel van on the second rung that, if it hadn't already been stripped, definitely would. He was three steps toward the stacks when he heard a starchy, barking voice behind him in a language he didn't know. Bogdan, steps away, told him in a low whisper to turn around and be calm, be calm.

A white light shined over them. Pax mimicked Bogdan and raised his hands aloft, seeing the dim profile of a man behind a flashlight. The man was wearing a uniform and held a rifle at them. Bogdan was saying a lot of slow, methodical words in something like Ukrainian but not, and Pax homed in on the one uttered that he could maybe fathom.

"Rosiys'kyy." Russki, he thought. Russian.

Bogdan began gesturing at the soldier to lower his gun, which earned more heavy barks. The Russian's words were slurring and the shock was passing and Pax's eyes were adjusting to the white light. It dawned on him that the man must not have a radio, otherwise he would've already used it. He was about ten feet away. Pax doubted very much the enemy would be able to get off two accurate shots in that time, not without night vision. He felt the heel of the pistol in his pocket against his hip.

There was a sound of crunching gravel behind the Russian. Then the man was gasping, hissing for air. The flashlight fell to the ground. On instinct Pax darted away and he glimpsed Bogdan doing the same, the other direction. He took cover behind an old refrigerator on its side. His eyes flitted about for comprehension as his ears found the clear and evident throes of a man being strangled. A couple minutes later, he heard his name.

"Corporal Paxton. We are good now."

The colossal shape of Unknown emerged as Pax returned to the area in front of the metal stacks. A body lay in the mud crumpled in the fetal position. It wore a digital-flora uniform and a helmet with big goggles and a patch on its shoulder was smeared with the letter Z, one stroke in white, the middle in blue, the last in red. Pax saw that it was a man about his age, about his build, an open liquor bottle wedging out of a pants pocket. Bogdan had already claimed its rifle. Unknown sneered and said "Veselka" to it. Then he sucked in air through his nose and spat as hard as he could downward.

Pax thumbed the beads on his wrist and managed out a singular "How?"

"I follow," Unknown said. It was enough of an answer to cease any next question.

Bogdan clicked his red-lens light. Pax took the cue. The totaled minivan had full, near-pristine bowels, complete with a long water pump fitted for a big-block engine. It took a few minutes but Pax wrenched it free, then held the perfect little thing between his palms. It was about eight pounds of cool cast aluminum. They began moving back toward the chain-link fence. More machine-gun fire lashed away in the far black. Pax heard the sludge of the brook.

The three men walked the bank in silence. As they approached the village road, Bogdan stopped midstride and knelt. In succession, Pax and Unknown did the same. A trio of red flares severed the night above. Their glow brought new sight. Some sort of armored personnel carrier now sat parked at the cottage at the bend of the road. It had eight wheels and a pointed nose and a raised autocannon. Pieces of masking tape marked its side with a *Z*.

They waited and watched. Nothing stirred around the carrier. The only sound Pax could identify was water running in the brook. Bogdan rose like a thief and motioned with his fingers for them to hustle past, one at a time. A gunshot came from the cottage. It was followed by a woman's resonant scream.

Bogdan repeated himself through the dark with his fingers. Unknown shook his head emphatically and gestured to the cottage. They both looked at Pax. He was their third. He held the tiebreaking vote.

Pax bowed his head in thought, feeling the pistol in one fleece pocket, the water pump in the other. Then he stood and began striding toward the cottage.

Halfway there more star clusters entered the sky. To his immediate front, adjacent to the carrier and against the side of the cottage, were two bodies, one on top of another. One wore a military uniform. The other was protesting, in voice and body. The man with the uniform looked up, seeing them in return. The world unplugged again. When the next flare burst, the shadowy glint of a long rifle barrel pointed their way, searching the night.

When in doubt, move, Lee and the infantry had taught

him, so that's what Pax did, angling toward the carrier. But he'd hesitated, staggered a bit, too, while Unknown ran direct, a frontal assault. Pax raised his pistol out and up, but it was clumsy, because there was nothing to aim at, only rambling darkness, and then there was a noise like wood planks slapping together, and when more star clusters entered the sky, Pax saw a large form collapsed to his periphery and he knew what was next, so he picked the streak of shadow against the cottage that was tinted different and fired a controlled pair into it, center mass.

A red light seized the bend of the roadside. Pax stared into it, then along it. The man in the uniform was folded into the ground. He'd been shot in the chest multiple times and looked very dead. Pax traced the source of the light. Bogdan lowered the rifle he'd taken from the first soldier in the junkyard. It appeared they'd found the man together. Shouting emerged from the cottage. Bogdan turned, raised his rifle again, and fired point-blank into the skull of another Russian hurrying through the cottage doorway. Then the recruiter yelled into the home, barking out hostile commands Pax didn't need to know to understand.

Pax crawled to Unknown, who was trying to rise, failing at it. A torrent of blood ran from the man's throat over his thick beard and neck. "You badass," Pax told him. "That was fucking badass, you know that?" The bushy man dug into the dirt beside him with his fingers and nails and clasped a measure of earth. He died while Pax was ripping apart his own undershirt to try to apply a tourniquet. Pax's hands were sopped in blood and mud and there was nothing to be done. He sat there next to the body, only half paying attention as Bogdan returned with two people, a child and a fat old man.

"Found them hiding in the closet. No more vatniks."

"What about that shot?"

"The grandmother." Bogdan plucked at his beard. "She is—" He clacked his tongue against the back of his mouth.

The local woman wouldn't come near them. The old man went to her while Bogdan spoke with the child, a girl about nine or ten. She answered something in the affirmative, pointing toward a tree line away from the road. The girl's mother or sister—Pax was trying to give the courtesy of not looking that way—pulled her in for an embrace. There was a muffled exchange. Then the three locals slipped into the night.

"They good?" Pax was still on the ground next to the dead man.

"There is a neighbor with a heated cellar. They say they will go there and hide."

Bogdan approached and closed the body's jaw and eyelids. Then he crossed the man's arms over his heart and said something in Ukrainian. It could've been a prayer. It could've been a vow.

"We must move," he said. "The gunfire may bring more."

They walked the edge of the road mostly in silence. Pax interrupted it only once.

"We could've reached Odesa without this," he said by the farmhouse. "This is my fault."

"Nonsense." Bogdan looked up and off the road toward the shelled building, pausing to let pass a brittle gust of wind. "We all make our choices."

They continued, hearing more firing behind them. Pax searched for the tree with the animal with translucent eyes. Either it had departed or had never been there. As they rounded the corner to the clinic, Bogdan shouted, "Veselka!" Roman stepped forward from the doorway holding his shotgun. Bogdan gripped the younger man's shoulder and went to speak with the nurse.

Pax set to work on replacing the water pump. Roman lingered in the courtyard, then began pacing it.

"Is Unknown coming back?"

"No."

A minute passed, maybe longer.

"We didn't even know his real name."

Pax focused on the engine.

They decided to leave with the first tinges of sun, light scratching at the eastern sky. Bogdan couldn't drive because of his legs. Roman couldn't operate a stick shift. Svitlana wanted to sit in the back with Taras, so that left Pax to assume the wheel. The adrenaline from the long night had dispersed and the comedown beckoned and he wanted desperately to sleep. Two hours was nothing, he reminded himself, just two hours to Odesa. Roman pulled an energy drink from his messenger bag and handed it to him.

"Last one," he said.

Pax opened the can and drank from it and looked into the breaching sky. He saw clouds, fat, puffy ones, which he was grateful for. Cloudy days tended not to be cruise-missile days. And had spring come? It felt like it might have. Two hours is nothing, he thought again.

He powered on his phone to text Merriman. "Got to tomorrow," he wrote.

His former captain replied in seconds. "My man. Stay dangerous."

They wheeled Taras out on a gurney. His beard had been trimmed and his bald head was covered with a knit beanie. He was wrapped in so many blankets Pax couldn't see the state of his wound. He held both of Svitlana's palms to his chest but insisted on shaking hands with each of the men who'd come to help.

"Duzhe dyakuyu," he said to Pax.

"English," Svitlana said.

"Thank you." His grip was weak and clammy, and the pallid face and the distant tone revealed a man deep in anesthetics. "We are now brothers."

Pax didn't know what to say so he nodded vaguely and took back his hand.

Svitlana grabbed his elbow at the driver's door.

"Luke," she said.

"Gypsy."

"I lied to you." He tilted his head. Here it comes, he thought. She kissed his cheek with dry, chapped lips and said, "'In the Aeroplane Over the Sea' was my favorite song."

"I fucking knew it."

"The best listener. Who forgets nothing."

She smiled. Pax smiled back.

"Do something for me, okay? Be kinder to yourself."

He nodded and said he would.

He kept the van to a slow crawl as they navigated through the village. There had not been any gunfire or star clusters for more than an hour and the nurse had told them that the radio station in Mykolaiv said the Russians were withdraw-ing from the city. They just needed to get across the river and on the road to Odesa. It was a straight shot from there.

Roman saw the tank first as they neared the initial round-about. It was small and drab green and rushing away from them, eastbound. Pax stopped on the side of the road and waited, holding his breath and remembering seeing the car-casses of Soviet tanks in Afghan boneyards, wondering what they looked like in the wild. Lethal, he thought. That's the answer. The tank's gun was scanning the road to its front and all Pax could do was pray it didn't angle back their way and it didn't. Soon the Z-tank passed beyond their line of sight. He let himself exhale just as Bogdan tapped his leg and pointed through his side window.

"They've already seen us. Drive slow. I will talk us past. If I say rainbow, you push that accelerator to hell."

A checkpoint now stretched through the second round-about. They'd turned the empty fountain into an open-air storage depot. Bright white flashlights signaled at them through the dim of the morning. Pax saw the Russian flag affixed to another pointed-nose armored carrier, single strands of concertina wire laid over both sections of the road. Amateur shit, he thought, barely better than nothing. He squinted and saw four, perhaps five human silhouettes milling around. Maybe a lieutenant in the carrier with a radio, too, he thought, maybe one more orc in the cupola on the machine gun. Everything was so murky it was hard to be definitive about anything his eyes registered. He moved the van forward as slow as he could without being obvious about it.

The flashlights grew less urgent as they approached the checkpoint. The armored carrier lurked to his immediate left; if he rolled down his window and reached out, he'd be able to touch its hull. Bogdan cracked open his and answered commands in terse, neutral Russian. Two of the soldiers had their rifles slung but two others held theirs at the low-ready. Pax could hear Roman's leg trembling against the back of his seat. He sought out Svitlana in the rearview mirror. She looked forward, holding the hands of her supine husband.

One of the Russians was trying to get Bogdan out of the van. They want him to open the back, he thought. That's what I'd do if I were them. He scanned the roundabout. The dismounted soldiers had all gathered on the right of the van, where Bogdan played dumb. The razor wire on that side had been strung out to its full length, but on his side, where the inbound flow berthed, it lay incomplete. It'd be tight but I can get around it, he thought. The angle's sharp but doable.

He'd already made the decision as Bogdan hissed "Veselka!" from his seat.

"Down, down!" he shouted, wishing he'd had the where-withal to tell people to minimize themselves beforehand, his foot all the way down on the accelerator with his body tucked into the fold of the seat so only the top of his head cleared the dashboard as his hands held the very bottom of the steering wheel. A rip of what sounded like hail hit along the side of the van and shattered out his window but he was driving, and Bogdan was shouting "Go, go, go!" and Svitlana shouting the same, and there was more hail, but he was still driving. He glanced in the rearview mirror again and saw nothing, no one following, and beyond nothing were the stirs of a new sun, a new day, and he was still driving, and he heard Roman screaming about glass, and his arm, and blood, but he was still driving, and Bogdan was cackling now, deranged and ju-bilant, and he was still driving, and he heard Svitlana saying, "We're clear!" and her voice was beautiful and strong, and he was still driving.

He sat back up his seat and felt a wrenching between his ribs and armpit. Then the wrenching was all over the side of his body, and Bogdan seized the wheel from his seat and was shouting, spittle shooting from his mouth and over his beard. Pax tried to move his foot to the brake but couldn't. He tried again but couldn't again. Then he lifted his good leg with his good arm, flinging it onto the far pedal, and he couldn't feel it land but he did sense the motion of the van slowing under the power of the action. He kept himself very still and ponderous until he was certain they'd stopped.

A tremendous agony beyond anything he'd ever known was annihilating his capacity to think. He twisted himself back over, so he could hear, so he could see. His body bayed with more agony. Bogdan was clasping his hand. He looked again to the rearview mirror where daylight stirred, hoping for a pair of olive eyes to hold with his own.

X

Svitlana didn't think she'd ever seen Lviv from this approach, certainly not at this hour. A city of hills and tumbling angles, it looked fresh under the light of dawn, even enchanted. She could just make out the top of Castle Hill from the highway, horizontal bands of blue and yellow crowning it. Beneath that, she knew, ran the cobblestone streets of the old town, where squads of boys ran around shooting toys at one another, hers among them.

She'd grown up resenting Lviv for no other reason than it was home. She'd left as soon as she could, returning only when she'd had nowhere else to go. It was so pompous, she'd once thought, and it was. It was too modern for the rest of her country, she'd thought, and it was, and it was too shabby for the rest of Europe, she'd thought, and it was. It comforted and it suffocated and it sustained and it held back. It presented as an open place of culture but could be just as traditional and conservative as any of the villages. It'd taken her years to understand that Lviv could be both those things, wholly and truly, and that the discrepancies therein were what made it most interesting of all.

Would they stay? She wasn't yet sure. She wanted so many things for her son, more than any one place in the world could provide. More than the world itself could. But Denys was at an age when he needed his father, and his father was here. His father would remain here, too, a martial spirit had overtaken Taras that his brush with death had only seemed to amplify. The surgery had gone well. All that now lay between him and home was a couple weeks' recovery at the hospital in Odesa, even if his blathering roommate might not leave him alone. Before they'd left, Roman had been asking the doctors what the scars on his shoulder and arm would look like after the bandages got removed.

The war had trapped her. It had trapped them all. She looked at her hand on the steering wheel and the strange, chipped prayer beads wrapped around her wrist.

Bogdan sat in the passenger seat, staring out the window, dark bags under his eyes. He'd ignored her when she told him to sleep. The body lay in a coffin in the back of the van. Two of his countrymen awaited them in the city. The officer who promised to escort Luke home to America. And the news correspondent who promised to make his story famous.

"I don't think that ever mattered to him," she'd said.

"Perhaps not," Bogdan had replied. "But it'll matter to Ukraine. Heroyam slava."

She wasn't sure she understood why Luke Paxton had come. She wasn't sure she'd ever understand. He'd bled out between them on the highway, gasping and twitching, his hands and cheeks frigid cold. He kept trying to speak, over and over, and it'd been Bogdan who'd pulled a word from the convulsions and gore.

"He's saying 'Lee.'"

She'd failed at so many things in life. She'd failed so many people, as well. But she'd done well in that moment, she knew she had. She'd given him that.

"He's good, Luke," she'd said, holding him as he shook, refusing away any tears, forcing herself to smile downward, watching the color in his face wash out. "He's good and safe and so are you, you are good and you are safe, you are good and you are safe. You are good, Luke, and you are safe, you are good and you are safe."

The others had said he was already gone. But she knew he'd heard her.

Acknowledgments

This novel would not have been possible without many wise and lovely human beings I've been blessed to know. They include draft readers Adrian Bonenberger, Jenny Croft, Jack Douglass, Annie Gallagher, Deborah Scott Gallagher, Phil Klay, Ryan Elliott Smith, and Corey Sobel.

Much gratitude to Adrian Bonenberger, Benjamin Busch, Jeremy Fisher, Nazar Guzar, William McNulty, Iryna Solomko, Adam Tsou, "Daniela," Mykyta, T1, T3, and the many others I met, interviewed, or worked alongside in Ukraine. Thank you for your examples and friendship.

Molly Atlas is simply the best agent in the business. Thank you. My editor, Natalie Hallak, saw the best version of this story well before I did, and guided me to it. Thank you. Elizabeth Hitti, Gena Lanzi, Lindsay Sagnette, and many others at Atria Books have worked hard on this book and championed it. Thank you.

Thank you to Carolyn Sickles and the Tulsa Artist Fellowship, and Dr. Adam Long and Shannon Williams of the Hemingway-Pfeiffer Museum, for providing those most sacred things for any writer, time and space. Thank you to Eric Sullivan, Kelly Stout, Michael Sebastian, and *Esquire* for letting me go forth and figure out the story while I'm there.

In addition to my own reporting in Ukraine, this novel was deeply informed by the work of other journalists, to include Francis Farrell, Yevheniia Motorevska, Illia Ponomarenko, Zakhar Protsiuk, Oleksiy Sorokin, and the entire team at the *Kyiv Independent*; the late Victoria Amelina, who died in July 2023 from injuries sustained in a Russian missile attack on a restaurant in eastern Ukraine; Sarah Ashton-Cirillo, Mac William Bishop, Thomas Gibbons-Neff, Danny Gold, Jake Hanrahan, Antonia Hitchens, Tim Judah, Ben Makuch, James Marson, and Sergio Olmos.

A phrase in this novel—"[It] made him feel like she was staring through him, into all the moral insecurity that growing up in a free country can instill"—is taken from an email my friend Mark Daily sent home in late 2006 from Iraq. I'd encourage anyone unfamiliar with Mark's life to seek out online his essay, "Why I Joined."

Some of the Judge's memories and experiences detailed in chapter IV are real-life anecdotes found in Artyom Borovik's tremendous account of the Soviet occupation of Afghanistan, *The Hidden War*.

Thank you to my family, my brother Luke, in particular, who not only lent his name to the novel's main character but also his everyday courage. Thank you to my sons, Samuel Edward and Jack Ramsey, and my wife, Annie, who deal with the challenges of living with a writer with grace and humor. I love you all very much.

To those I mentioned, and to the many others I didn't— sláinte.

About the Author

MATT GALLAGHER is a U.S. Army veteran and the author of the novels *Empire City* and *Youngblood*, a finalist for the Dayton Literary Peace Prize. His work has appeared in *Esquire, ESPN, The New York Times, The Paris Review*, and *Wired*, among other places. He's also the author of the Iraq war memoir *Kaboom*. A graduate of Wake Forest and Columbia, he is the recipient of the Tulsa Artist Fellowship, a Bread Loaf Writers' Conference Fellowship and a Sewanee Writers' Conference Fellowship and was selected as the 2022 Hemingway-Pfeiffer Museum Writer-in-Residence. Matt has traveled multiple times to Ukraine as both a volunteer and journalist. He lives with his family in Tulsa, Oklahoma.